HOW TO GET INTO
THE TWIN PALMS

A NOVEL BY
KAROLINA WACLAWIAK

TWO DOLLAR RADIO
Books too loud to ignore

TWO DOLLAR RADIO
Books too loud to ignore

TwoDollarRadio.com
twodollar@TwoDollarRadio.com

to my family

HOW TO GET INTO THE TWIN PALMS

IT WAS A STRANGE CHOICE TO DECIDE TO PASS

as a Russian. But it was a question of proximity and level of allure. Russians were everywhere in Los Angeles, especially in my neighborhood, and held a certain sense of mystery. I had long attempted to inhabit my Polish skin and was happy to finally crawl out of it. I would never tell my mother. She only thought of them as crooks and beneath us. They felt the same about us, we were beneath them. It had always been a question of who was under whom.

I SEE A COUPLE FROM THE TWIN PALMS FUCKING

against their car across the street from my apartment. I'm hiding behind the newly purchased ficus on my balcony and watching them. I wonder if they know each other and I want to know what he's whispering to her in Russian. I am a few feet away from them, in it with them, and I want to know if she's a *suka* or his wife. He wouldn't be fucking her like that if she were his wife. He grabs at her and she lets him touch her roughly and I wonder how he would touch me.

Is he a cab driver or a businessman?

He turns her around, face toward the car and pushes her against it. He moves his hand in between her legs and pulls one up around him. She doesn't hesitate.

I whistle. He stops breathing and says something in Russian that I can't understand. I lean forward, trying to hear better, still hidden behind the bush. It doesn't matter. I'm not hidden enough and he sees me. The woman says something to me in Russian, spits on the ground, pulls down her dress, and pulls up her panties.

He buckles his belt. Zips. They walk quickly back to the Twin Palms and I sit outside on my balcony, hoping to see more but no one else comes out to fuck from the Twin Palms tonight.

If you walked by the Twin Palms during the day you would surely miss it. The doors are green and it looks like a rundown relic of old Los Angeles. The sign is yellow with a drawn on palm tree. The cabs are gone and the street is empty, clean of cigarette butts.

I want to get inside the Twin Palms. I want them to ask me what I am. So I wait for the cabs to come back, for the Russians to swarm back like birds.

The stores on Fairfax are called *apteka* and sell prosthetic body parts and humidifiers and medicine that I have never seen before. They are next to the grocery stores that sell aging fruit and herring and halvah. I hate herring. In tubs with oil and onions, the silvery pieces curl onto each other, unmoving. I should love herring. I should love borscht. I should slurp it up with pumpernickel or rye.

As I walk down the street the smell overwhelms me. The smell of rye bread and *ponchki* filled with prune jam. The yeast smell from the bakery overtakes everything and keeps it an immigrant neighborhood in Los Angeles.

There are Russians and Ukrainians on my street. They are not like the Russians in the Twin Palms. They wear plastic shoes and stand with their socks pulled up. The men wear shorts and their bellies hang down and out of their yellowing undershirts. The women weep. The men yell. I see them watching me through their crocheted curtains, waiting to see who comes in and who comes out of my apartment. Picking the ones I should be ashamed of.

The next night something is happening in the Twin Palms and everyone going inside is dressed in fur. I want to really see them so I lean up close to the women in their coats as I walk through and feel the silver foxes and minks brush against my cheek. The coats smell like the one my mother used to have, the one I wanted. It was a silver fox and she used to wear it all the time in Poland when she was young. The age I am now. My grandmother had a fur too.

A sign of a good husband in Poland is one who puts you in a silver fox – short or long. Long is better. More exclusive.

The women in the fox furs don't appreciate how close I am to them, how my face touches the scruff of their arm. The mink of their sleeve. They curse me in Russian. *Suka*. Bitch. In Polish, bitch is *kurwa*… coorvaaah, but could also be a whore. Was *suka* a whore too? Who else but a whore would rub her cheek against their furs? I watch them walk up the stairs and want to follow.

I round the corner and hear the sound wafting down the street. *Suka. Suka. Suka.* The women go upstairs. The men stay behind. Smoke. Snuff out cigarettes.

I try passing again.

The men stare at me in their black leather dusters. With their Eastern Bloc homemade haircuts – a custom they never gave up in America. Hair falling in between linoleum squares, beside refrigerators, ovens, the missed unswept tufts accumulating. I catch their eyes and know they wonder what I am. If I am one of them. Most of them have gray hairs weaving through those homemade haircuts. They watch my 25-year-old ass move, tight and upright in my black stretch pants, as I walk past them slowly. I want to get up there so I walk even slower. I know what they want to ask. *Polska? Ruska? Svedka?* Or maybe just *Amerykanska.* They can't tell with me.

They won't ask, instead they stare; whisper something to see if I turn. Flick ash near me to see if I quicken my pace. They want to know if I'm used to men like them. I keep moving slowly because I want to see if it's working. They look at my ass, my tits, my face last. I turn my head and stare up the stairs into the Twin Palms. The walls are mirrored and I see the women without their furs, in silk and pearls and amber, their hair in root vegetable colors, their false teeth, metal wires showing between molars. I know some of them used to be village girls back in the old country. I can tell.

I lurk behind the community center and watch the cabbies start to circle again. They park. They stand outside of the Twin Palms and wait for the doors to open. They smoke. They laugh. They speak only in Russian. I stare at them and try to decide which one I would take on in order to get upstairs. They are a mix of young and old and the young look rough, like they've just arrived. Their leather dusters have a still-new sheen to them, bought with their first paycheck from the cabstand. Would becoming one of their girlfriends even get me upstairs?

I have to watch them closely. Who goes up. Who stays down. Who has a wife. Who is alone.

More people come. Do I want to wait for better Russians to come or should I try my luck with these? If I am going to spend my time at the Twin Palms I want it to be frequent. I want them to know me. I want to pass fully. What will my name be? I will have to change the *I* to *Y*. I will have to get my story straight.

THERE ARE 20,000 BABY NAMES IN THE

book I purchased from the store that has menorahs in the window and Russian paperbacks in the back. The most popular Russian baby names are as follows:

Sasha – spelled Sasha and Sascha. Both make the list.
Karina
Aleksandra
Calina
Anya
Nadya
Agnessa
~~Romochka~~

I wasn't sure if the last name was a girl's or boy's so I cut it off the list immediately.

They were all acceptable choices – all ending with *A* and having the same Eastern European feel. I wanted my *Y* to be prominent. Anya. It could pass for Polish or Russian. I could move easily with it. Fluidly.

I practiced speaking with an accent, but it just sounded like all the times I would mock my mother's thick Polish accent. *Beach* sounded like *bitch*, *count* like *cunt*. I sounded like a crude carica-ture of her, my voice low and thick, rolling the R's. I could play her for humor but I could never be her, really. I switched back to my flat American accent and gave up. I was from nowhere and I had lived in too many places to hold on to anything permanent in my voice.

I HAD INHERITED THE APARTMENT FROM

someone I once knew and it was strange to live here, to think about what he had done in here. The apartment was vertical blinds, beige carpets, bare off-white walls, and small things I found that people left behind.

Bobby pins in the corner of the bedroom carpet, a hair ball of long blond hair in the living room that the vacuum had missed, six shrimp-flavored Ramen noodle packages at the back of the kitchen cabinet, and purple Fabuloso floor cleaner, untouched.

I used the bobby pins, threw away the hair, pushed the Ramen aside, and filled the cabinets with my own food. I threw away the floor cleaner and bought myself Ajax powder, like my mother always used.

The apartment was rent controlled so I wasn't going to complain. But, I was curious about whose hairball was in the living room. I thought maybe some kind of actress-to-be. The roots were dark brown. She was in need of a touch-up, whoever she was, and her hair was fine, like mine.

I considered keeping the hair, saving it, but I was already holding on to too much.

SOMETIMES, WHEN THERE IS NO PARKING ON

Fairfax the Russians park on my street. The men are always alone, having already deposited their wives or significant others curbside at the Twin Palms. Alone, they like to look. I can giggle and coo here without being called a *suka* or worse, *shalava*. Here, I can woo freely.

I usually sit behind my ficus and wait. I see a few pull up with their Cadillacs and Buicks. These are better Russians. Better than the cabbies. They are well fed and wear their shirts unbuttoned two buttons to show their chest hair, their lion's mane. I whistle from my ground-level balcony. They look for a moment, or two. I'm not their type or I'm not their girl or I just don't work because they keep walking.

My neighbor climbs out of the sliding glass door and starts preparing something. He lays down newspaper on the table outside. He brings a floor lamp from inside the apartment outside. He brings out a few knives, and finally a fish. He smiles at me. His mustache is fine haired and ill groomed. He does not have gray yet.

He shakes his knife at me. "Do you want to take a try?" He points to the fish and smiles.

"Gut it?"

"Yes, gut and scale. Easy work." He laughs at this but I don't. His English is thick with an accent. His mother still cuts his hair in the bathroom. I can see it. The lopsided cuts. The cowlick. The telltale sign of a homemade haircut. His mother only speaks to me in Russian and I do not understand. She comes outside and smiles at me. She wants me to gut the fish and motions to it. She wants me to like her son.

He is much older than me. But still not old.

He lives across the street and walks back and forth. One day he talks to me – more than hello and goodbye.

"My mother thinks you're pretty," he says.

I stare at him. I'm not sure how to react so I smile and shrug.

"She said it. I didn't."

"Tell her thank you."

I smile at her and she smiles back with her few silver teeth, just like my grandfather. Her single son climbs into her ground-level balcony every day, pulls open the sliding glass door and goes inside. A few minutes later he comes back out the front door with a small bag of garbage and brings it to the dumpster. Every day.

Why not use the front door each time? It was some kind of strange ritual I did not understand. I never considered scaling my balcony to press through my sliding glass. We were supposed to be cultured here and not do those kind of things in this country. Or call attention to ourselves. I wasn't sure why he didn't know that in America we used the front door, always.

My neighbor's son doesn't go to the Twin Palms. He walks around the streets with his white athletic socks pulled up high, and black, plastic sandals. And shorts. The men who go to the Twin Palms do not wear shorts. They wear slacks and silk shirts unbuttoned and leather jackets even if the Santa Ana winds are roaring.

I WORK HARD ON MY APPEARANCE. I GO TO A

neighborhood salon. The women have curlers in their hair and are all over 50. They will leave the salon with plastic wrapped around their perms so the curl sets properly. I sit in a chair and stare at my hairdresser. I brought a picture from *Burda*, the only magazine I know of that is for both Polish and Russian women. I can't read the words but am transfixed by the Cyrillic. The women are smiling and wearing their versions of American styles. I point to the picture. The hair is dark, a maroon tint to it, and much darker than the carefully highlighted mane I have spent years cultivating. She comes back with a tub full of color and brushes it on. She rolls it atop my head and clips it.

"Come to dryer."

I follow her and look at myself in the mirror as the machine hums. When she washes my hair I notice the dye has stained the skin all around my hairline. My ears. My skin has dark splotches to match my new dark strands. I will have to spend hundreds of dollars to go back to the careful blond.

"Do you like?"

"It's dark."

"Yes, moody. Like picture."

I stare at myself. My eyes are glowing. My hair flat and black, not dark chestnut. With a hint of maroon. Whatever it is, I will have to work with it.

I keep whistling at the Russian men and so far that has not worked. I spend evenings walking back and forth past the Twin Palms. Now some of the men nod at me from the front and stare at my ass from the back. My new slim black pants accentuate my hips and elongate my legs. They seem to like that. My dark hair makes my eyes more cat-like and brighter in hue. More Eastern European. Less American. I am starting to make sense to them. I am taking off all my American skin. Killing my ability to pass for Middle American and quiet and from here. Instead I am from the *bloki* again. Soviet-built and dooming.

WHEN I SEE HIM I KNOW IT'S GOING TO BE HIM.

He is not exceptionally tall, not exceptionally anything. He is nondescript in the Eastern European way. The Soviet way. Brown, muddled hair, like deerskin. He is beginning the slant toward overweight.

I watch him walk toward the Twin Palms and I know he'll appreciate all the work I have put in. Should I yell to him in words I have just learned or speak to him in English? I panic and speak English. More of a grunt than a sentence. Something vague about the weather. The street. I catch him off guard. I wonder if women ever talk to him. If they ever come on to him. He is not the man I saw outside pressed up against his car, against a woman. He is new, fresh and I know I can hold onto his attention for a while.

"It's street cleaning today. You'll get a ticket," I said. He stares at me blankly.

"You can't park on that side on Tuesdays and Fridays between 12 and 2 and you can't park on this side Mondays and Thursdays. From 1 to 3."

"Who says?"

I point to the signs. "The city."

He shrugs his shoulders.

"Do you understand?"

He looks at me, inspecting me really. My hair, my eyes. The

signs of who I am and where I am from, if he wants to talk to me or deal with me or if I am just another American. He has a clean haircut. A barber cut, or even a salon. Not from the kitchen, over a basin with fine brown hairs dropping on peeling linoleum. He's slack-jawed and has pocket eyes, blue or green or something in between. Like a shark.

"Fuck them."

He walks away, down the street and toward the Twin Palms. He doesn't turn around to see if I'm still watching him. He's older than me, probably in his late 30's. I pull the dead leaves off my ficus. It's not taking to the dips in temperature at night.

When my Russian comes back there is a ticket on his car and he says a string of words in his brusque language and stares at me like I'm supposed to know. I blush, get nervous. He calls to me in his accented English and asks me if I saw them do it.

I say no.

"You should have listened to me. I think." I say it with a smirk. He looks up, taken by surprise.

"What's your name?"

I tell him it's Anya. A good, strong Eastern Bloc name. I watch him move toward me.

He stares up at my apartment building. Satellites hanging off every balcony. He asks me if I live here. I tell him yes. And then he asks me what I wanted him to ask me.

I pause and wonder what I should say. If I should tell him the truth or if I should tell him what he wants to hear.

"Do you think I'm Russian?" I counter.

He says something to me in Russian. Something I can't comprehend completely, maybe a word or two, but said so quickly it just sounds like a scramble. He has his answer, I am not. He stares at me, looks me up and down. "So, what are you then?" he asks.

I hesitate, I can be anything, but I revert to some kind of small pride. "Polish," I say.

He cocks his head, like he knew all along and was putting me through the motions. He says something to me in Polish. Now I can understand: "Polish girls are very beautiful. Almost like Russians."

I blush in the way you blush at an insult. I have named myself to him now. "Have you been to the Twin Palms?" I ask.

"Yes," he says and laughs.

"What's it like?"

"Not for girls like you."

"What kind of girl is that?"

He stares at me and starts backing away. And as he does I know exactly what kind of girl that is. He turns and walks back to his car and I already want to see him again.

I ask him what his name is.

"Lev."

He doesn't even smile.

WHAT I AM IS ALWAYS THE FIRST QUESTION.

Since the camps. Since always. One camp was in Austria when I was very small, after we left our village and before my father began to fear everything. While we waited for a country to take us, Reagan became our hero. While he worked hard to stamp out Communism, he let us sneak in on a Pan Am flight.

I was sent to the other camp when I was eleven.

Bandera, Texas.

Camp Rainbow was a camp for immigrant children, a place where we could learn to be American. We took classes like arts and crafts and classes about appropriate assimilation and learned about MTV. American pop culture. I already knew about it. I danced hungry like the wolf.

I never wanted to be a good Polish girl.

When I was young in Texas, the woman across the street had a snake hose that flailed around, sending water sailing through the air. Her yard was still brown and I had a hard time trying not to get wet as I walked up the steps to knock on her door.

She knew my mother. She felt bad for us. Our threadbare clothing, church donated in black bags, broken-armed dolls. She fed me American things.

My favorite things:

<u>Wonder Bread</u> – I liked to touch it, watch the white bounce back from my fingertips.

<u>Margarine</u> – I didn't know what it was but it was a bright yellow that looked like egg yolks and slid across the Wonder Bread without ripping it.

<u>Sugar</u> – I had it sprinkled on top of Wonder Bread and margarine. The sandwich had to have the edges neatly pinched together so not a granule was lost. My neighbor did this for me but it was also important for me to reinforce the creases myself.

I always ate these sandwiches hungrily. It was my favorite thing. A bread, butter, and sugar sandwich. I snuck away to her house, dust-covered fake foliage in every corner. She fed me sandwich after sandwich and I was careful not to lose a granule. The layer of sugar crunched in my mouth. If I lost a bit on her stoop, while sitting there eating it, I'd take my finger, stick it in my mouth, wet it and run it along the concrete, picking up the sugar and sticking it back in my mouth.

My mother didn't know about my bread, butter, and sugar sandwiches.

We ate *galaretka* at our house. Things little girls did not like. I picked the pieces of dill off of my potatoes and checked the refrigerator daily, hoping one day there would be a tub of margarine. There never was.

But, I wasn't off the boat anymore, like these people. The second wave of immigrants from Poland, Russia, Laos, Cambodia. We couldn't speak to one another. They were too fresh. We slept on bunk beds and were told to watch out for scorpions, water moccasins in the river, tarantulas in the trees.

I ate sliced pickles from a jar every meal for two weeks and lost 15 pounds. My father said I looked like an escapee from a concentration camp. I thought I looked slim and tan and newly American. I kissed a Polish boy there. His name was Poitr and his face was covered in red pustules. I felt them on his back too, when I rubbed at his shirt. I felt one pop. He always wore black shirts. Even in the Texas sun. Piotr gave me presents of N.W.A tapes and the N.W.A hat he was so proud of, the red stitching of the letters bursting from black fabric.

He stuck his tongue in my throat and jabbed it around. Hit my teeth. I giggled and he kept asking me what was so funny. I wanted him to hurry up and finish. I told him I was fourteen and he was already sixteen and I wanted him to put his hand under my shirt but he was scared. He was not a man.

I left him on the picnic tables, alone, and went looking for someone older. Someone less scared. Later, I would put the hat over my face and inhale, play the tape in my boom box, and try to remember him.

I tried to look beautiful for the American camp counselors but they didn't understand us. They just shoved us together, in the pool, at dances. Told us how we were supposed to act now, swaggering. Accent-less, unlike our parents. We still had a chance in this country, we could still pass.

I had been in America longer than the rest of these children. Mimicry is what I was good at. I observed and made practiced movements, keeping quiet so that I could listen. It pleased me to know I *could* do these things. American things like shout *cocksucker* as a punctuation mark, gyrate my pelvis wildly to Duran Duran's "Hungry Like The Wolf" while mouthing the words "*I'm on the hunt I'm after you*," and saunter around the bone-dry landscape as if drunk, as if I were some kind of John Wayne. It didn't matter that I didn't know what these things were, just that I was free to do them with no one to stop me.

LOS ANGELES HAS ONE POLISH CHURCH.

Catholic, of course. On West Adams. I went there when Pope John Paul died and everyone was sobbing. The mass was in Polish and I could pick out lines and prayers that I had learned when I was a child. Still learning Polish. Still learning English. On one side of the altar hung a large photograph of the deceased Pope. It had no doubt been affixed to the wall when John Paul became Pope. On the other side, a copy of the Black Madonna.

The Black Madonna of Częstochowa, Poland, has a cut on her cheek and a golden crown and holds her son. Her cheek was sliced by the Hussites in the 1400s and it bled. We worship the painting and we worship the scar. I have crawled on my knees in front of her image in Poland.

She is surrounded by reminders of sickness. Hanging crutches, small crosses worn around the neck of the sick and dying, miraculously cured. All the cured leave the remnants of their maladies all around her in the Jasna Góra Monastery where she is worshiped. She is the mother of God and an image of her hangs in every good Polish person's house.

There is also only one Polish store and two Polish restaurants in Los Angeles. Sausages hang on the walls of the store. The older women do not speak English. The younger ones look bored and tired and don't want anything to do with me. I am nothing to them. A strange in between. They grunt at me when I try and place my order in their language. Behind them hang kielbasas; thin and long, short and fat, in between sizes too. Blood sausages, hunter's sausage, white and special for Easter. Most have names that I cannot read so I point and sound out the words in my head, too shy to say them out loud. One day, maybe I will. Not today. I line the counter with sauerkraut I will never eat, and chocolates filled with plums that will get pushed to the back of the cupboard. Reminders of who I am, but who I am not quite.

Lev is waiting for me when I get home to my apartment. I think he is here for me because he's on my street again, in the same clothes I saw him in before. I want to smell him. Smell his smell. See if he smells like an immigrant or if he has become Americanized, slathering deodorant under his arms to mask the musk and the sweat and that smell that I find so intoxicating. Onions mixed with cheap cologne.

Once I smell him I won't have to ask how long he's been here.

He won't look at me. I'm pulling out the paper bags filled with sausages, tightly hidden behind white butcher paper to mask the smell. The prices are scrawled on the outside with black wax crayon. The fours and nines are curved differently. The twos have a different gait. As I linger I hear Lev clear his throat. I look up and attempt to act surprised. He asks me to watch his car, not let them ticket him this time and laughs at his own joke that I don't get.

"What's in there?" He points to my bag and I'm concerned that it's too invasive.

"*Kabanosy* and *kapusta*."

"Like a good Polish girl." He smiles his smile at me, his sneer.

I like that I have some pull with him. That I am not just American. That I am closer to him.

That is my trick.

"Do you want some?" I ask.

He pats his stomach. "I have to go upstairs. A party."

"What do they have up there?"

"Russians."

I smile at him and start walking away. Tell him I will, in fact, watch his car.

He laughs and tells me, "No, it was joke. I get someone else to make sure it's okay."

And then I know he's somebody. And then I know I want him even more.

In the morning, Lev's car is still there. I wonder who he went home with. If one of the fur-coated ladies drove him home or if he went with them, to their homes, to their apartments. Where he lives. If they went further east. Toward Little Armenia, where the other Russians live or if he traveled to the valley where the New Russian families live. The ones who moved here in the early '90s – the new flow.

A different man comes and moves Lev's car. He is lanky and disheveled and I watch him as he creeps into the front seat and patiently pulls back and forth, trying to get out of the tight spot. He swerves out in one final, impatient turn and drives down the street and disappears. After he moves the car there is shuffling in the apartments across the street. The men from Odessa begin to open doors, water plants. Come alive. It is morning and they are starting the routine of their day. Doing their chores so their wives will permit them to sit in lawn chairs, on their balconies, and watch the cars move back and forth down the street. Our buildings are all squat, two-storied, with balconies. All somewhat the same, tan stucco or white stucco or beige, fading into one another. Nondescript and unobtrusive, always striving to be mildly pleasant and to blend into the California landscape. But our block was different, house plants sitting outside, brightly beaded curtains haphazardly attached to the railing with butcher twine, and faded lace curtains in the windows.

We were still ethnic here. When people walked by, they would point at the windows and say things like, "Why are they drying their clothes outside? Aren't they afraid they'll get stolen?" No one's ever did. Not with Boris hanging out his window everyday, watching everyone go by.

I sit on my balcony and watch people get out of their cars and walk to the small shops on Fairfax and think things like, I was never a good girl, good enough to come back to. And, I want to be more permissive, unlike the wives on my street.

I can't though. I know myself.

I DIDN'T SEE LEV FOR A FEW WEEKS AFTER

that and I anticipated his return daily. Dreamt up our possible interactions. I learned new words in Russian. Things like: *Vsë tip-tóp!* And *kátit* in case he asked me how I was doing. Did they really mean, "It's all good"? I wasn't sure.

WHILE I WAITED FOR LEV TO RETURN I WENT

back to calling bingo numbers at the Protection of the Holy Virgin Russian Orthodox church. It was in Hollywood. I drove there and took Hollywood Boulevard to Argyle and stopped at the 7-Eleven nearby and always got a Cherry Coke. It was a long night there on Fridays and sometimes there were no breaks in between games. I also got a bag of Fritos. I hadn't had any in a while and it seemed right. They were the spicy kind. I thought the ladies would miss me but they didn't really. Someone else had started calling the numbers, a woman I knew. She only wore t-shirts with animals on them. Wolves, bears, sometimes dolphins. She wasn't happy about giving up her place to me. But I was the veteran here. I called the numbers slower and the old people had gotten used to the lilt in my voice. When they called me and told me the other woman wasn't working out, that I was the only person who could handle the ladies, I strong-armed the Holy Virgin into giving me $50 a game. I climbed onto the stage of the multi-purpose room and sat down next to the large illuminated sign covered in numbers lined across and bingo spelled out accordingly. I sat behind a box full of roiling bingo balls and watched the air pressure inside the box throw the numbered balls into a tornado. The tables were long and full of women. Mostly widows needing to get out, to forget that their husbands were dead and gone because they still had many, many years left to live. They had photos of their men as their lucky charms. Petite picture frames nestled next to small, childish objects. Plastic birds, broken timepieces, toy cars made by Mattel. They lined them up along the top edge of the bingo tables and spread the cards out in front of them. I began calling.

B 12.

And then another and then another. And then I heard the complaining beginning. The curled bouffants bobbing up and down. Pecking at the numbers with their ink blotters.

I was going too fast. They were grumbling and pecking and finally one called out, "What are you doing? You're going to fast! Have some mercy."

I slowed down. N 36. I drawled out the 6. I took a sip of Cherry Coke. My first of the night.

After Rosa Schwartzburg called "Bingo!" I called a break. There was a shuffling of cards. Dirty looks aimed at Rosa. She had not stopped her winning streak. Ten dollars and a Twizzler. Single stick. Not a pack. She was diabetic. I didn't understand the Holy Virgin sometimes. All these women were diabetic. Still with the Twizzlers every week. I walked down to the concession table and saw éclairs, hot dogs, and bags of potato chips. The low rent kind. A hot dog was $1.25. A hot dog with relish was $1.75. I found that to be outrageous. I ate it with mustard for $1.25. The ladies crowded around the table, calling out their orders. Frank, behind the table, couldn't keep up. His stomach brushed up against the chocolate on the top of the éclairs and stripped some off. No one noticed but me. The edges of the éclairs were now smeared and missing chocolate. I wanted one to top off the hot dog but I saw bits of Frank's shirt fuzz captured in the remaining chocolate and just couldn't do it. He smiled at me and winked. He thought I didn't notice, or maybe did and he wanted me to keep quiet about it. Once you got the ladies going there was no stopping them. I ran the numbers and he ran the stand and we were in this together. This Friday night at the Holy Virgin. Mary pushed up against me. She was wearing a Leonardo DiCaprio t-shirt. His face stretched large over her gigantic breasts.

"You're calling the numbers too fast," she said.

"I know. I heard all of you. I slowed down."

She scowled at me. "You don't have to be rude about it. Where have you been?"

I didn't really know what to tell her.

"Away on holiday with your boyfriend?" she continued.

"I don't have a boyfriend," I said.

"When I was your age I had six." She glared at me. Her face was round and her eyebrows overgrown. She had red lipstick on; smeared on account of the éclairs she had just eaten.

"I thought you were already married by my age."

"How old are you?"

"Twenty-five."

"Yeah, I was already married. And he was handsome. So handsome. He treated me like a princess. A doll."

"I'm sorry, Mary."

"You need sex. I need sex. Everyone needs sex."

This was a weekly thing and I was used to her frankness.

"I still need it. You think I don't have needs? I'm 82 and my libido is raging. Look at Carla. Ninety-two. She wants it."

I stared at Carla. She was small, hunched over, her curled bouffant was tilted with her head, a little to the left. I didn't think she still wanted it. But Mary called her over anyway. "Carla, how's your libido?"

I was starting to panic. I would have to call the numbers again in a second. The other women were getting restless.

"My what?" Carla stared at me. Her eyes said that she still wanted it.

"Libido. I said *libido*."

"My husband's dead. What am I going to do? Who cares?"

"The young ones are the ones I want. They can still get it up.

The old ones just squish." Mary smiled at me. "Get a young one. You don't want to feel the squish."

"All right, Mary. I'll try."

"You can't fuck? I can tell in your hips you can fuck." She shook her head at me as I walked away.

B 9.

They all stared at me and waited for me to call the next number. They held their blotters – shaking and salivating.

I HAD LEARNED FLIRTATIONS IN RUSSIAN WHILE

Lev was gone, but by the time I saw him again I had forgotten them all. My hair was growing out at the roots. I had given up making it into the Twin Palms. The women had stopped donning their fur coats as the weather became warmer and warmer. The bright days stretched longer and longer. They stomped around the sidewalk in silk and polyester. Bright knits in clashing patterns. They exposed their arms, wrinkled and sagging. The jewels on their hands could not obscure their aging fingers. With the furs gone they looked like immigrants again. Inexpensive fabrics and ill-fitting dresses and pant sets. The older women wore gauzy tops over satin shirts and covered the sag of their arms with volumes of sheer sleeves in melons and chartreuse. Their husbands and lovers clutched on to the fabric and led them upstairs. They were relics of the old world again. They were escaping the villages and gray Eastern Bloc high-rises the Soviets admired, our *bloki*.

When Lev parked again I was returning from Fairfax with a loaf of rye in my hand. He said something to me I couldn't understand, his accent newly thick. He repeated himself. Asked if he would get in trouble for parking here today. I told him I didn't know. Asked him where he had been, as if I had any claim to him. He didn't act surprised. He had been in Russia. I nodded. He was trying to shake off his accent again. Re-acclimate. He drew out his words carefully, overstated them, and asked how the weather had been. I had hoped we would have moved on to more probing topics. He stared at my hair, at the light strands coming in at the roots, making the dark brown look cheap, and fake. My dishwater blond was coming back. I quickly told him it had been hot here. Summer came early.

"In Russia it's still snowing."

After weeks of anticipation our meeting was underwhelming. Had he thought about me at all? I wanted to ask him where he went that last night. Who he had allowed to move his car in the morning. Who she was.

Instead, I said, "It must have been very cold."

He smiled and said, "Like Poland."

I smiled and nodded. Wanting him to say more so I could answer him.

"So it was good?" was all I could come up with.

He pulled out his buzzing cell phone and I saw the rings tattooed on his fingers. He smiled at me and turned away. Walked down the street.

He was a thief. A prisoner. He had black ink puckered in squares on his forefinger and pinky. How had I not seen them before? He looked back at me and waved as he walked away, toward the Twin Palms. It was the most attention he had ever paid me. He remembered me and remembered I was Polish. He looked thinner today. Younger. I had wished him back and he had come back.

ON WEEKDAYS I RUN FOUR MILES AROUND

the track at the high school across the street from the stores that sell Gefilte fish and latkes. I run and watch the old women push carts and pull groceries and go back to their apartments called The Hawaiian and The Tropical. They walk slowly, hunched over. One step at a time. Some wear *chustki* on their heads. Some just simple buns. They push and pull and walk down the street back home. My grandmother is doing this walk, in Poland. She leaves her tenement and makes the walk, past the decaying shops to the market. To buy small wild strawberries. Soups and potatoes. She carries the bags home, slowly, careful on the uneven sidewalks. She walks back to her empty apartment, the one room she occupies in the large apartment with high ceilings. Her room is crowded with crocheted tablecloths, photographs of us, small trinkets mismatched and misshapen, and her blaring television carefully tucked into the corner, directly opposite her sloping twin bed. She only watches American shows from the 1980s. Soap operas like *Santa Barbara*.

One man's voice is dubbed over the American shows and he is the voice of Polish TV. He does the men's voices and the women's voices. He does the children's voices. He does the voices of dogs and cats and birds. His voice is hypnotic.

I watch these old women in my neighborhood make this walk and I know that I never will, this old woman babushka walk. I will never wear a *chustka* on my head or put my swollen feet into perforated Eastern Bloc shoes with their American brand names. I will not crawl down the street, hunchbacked and slow. These are remnants of the old country and I am not that anymore. Or I never was.

They used to come to America, my grandparents. They took over our apartment in Poland, giving up their own village home because the Communists would only allow one dwelling per husband and wife. They took over our apartment in case we ever wanted to come back, in case America did not work out.

When they visited, it was always for a few months, and nearly every day they would wait for my parents to go to work and take out the old green Buick. My grandfather would pull it out of the driveway carefully, and my grandmother would put me in the backseat and beg me not to tell.

I never would. I would stick my head out the back window and pretend I was flying. My grandmother would play with the radio dials while my grandfather drove and looked out for police because what they were doing was not allowed. We would only drive around the block a few times but it felt like forever. I was free.

My grandfather taught me how to ride my bike.

My bike was pink and had tassels and it seemed much too big for me. He shouted commands at me in Polish as cars passed us and I wobbled. He had stuck the wooden handle of a broomstick in the back of the seat, above the wheel. He kept me riding in a line by holding on to it tightly. We lived in a brown-grassed cul-de-sac in Texas. Where the Air Force families lived. Not us, we were just immigrants. They were all transients and I never knew who most of them were, moving one year after another. We slowly rode past our house with the large Reagan/Bush poster in the front yard. It was red and white and blue, and most importantly, American.

When my grandfather let go of the broomstick handle I sailed down the street, felt the wind, felt the concrete beneath me and felt free for once. Until the pack of boys with the new and clean bikes saw me fly by, long broomstick handle bound to my bike, toothless grandfather trailing behind me. I felt my cheeks burn as they laughed, pointing at the broomstick, and I rounded the corner, falling out of sight.

"*Głupia!*" My grandfather came up and pulled me off the ground. I left him, my bicycle, and the broomstick on the street and ran for home.

MY UNEMPLOYMENT CHECK CAME EARLY THIS

week. I was going to try and make it last this time. I had to make sure I did not answer the phone between 9 and 7 if my mother called. As far as she knew I was still an employee of the FastTrak Employment Agency.

I had been a placement counselor and placed people in their temporary positions. I found people the right fit. I got a certain sense of pride when a temp hire became a full-time hire. It gave me a sense of accomplishment.

I had worn the same thing to work every day. Black slacks made from cheap synthetic fabric. Black or gray or white button down, with a bit of stretch. Black, sensible shoes. I tried to keep them unscuffed. I tried to keep my appearance neat. I understand the importance of looking good at work. When we first came to this country my mother went to work bra-less and without stockings. She was scolded by the owner's wife and made to wear a bra and nude stockings in the sweltering heat. She would come home and peel the stockings off her sweaty legs. She would tell me they said she looked too foreign, indecent. In America you couldn't show skin. You could not show your legs. You had to hide your skin with the appearance of skin, a bit browner than your own. I wanted to make sure my appearance was acceptable at work so I covered as much skin as possible. I wore collared shirts to cover my neck, as to not appear sexual or feminine. I was fired anyway. "Laid off" is what they called it. Our key client called and said I had sent them an inappropriate candidate. They were going over to Manpower Inc. That's what did it. Manpower Inc. Now I was getting a check on Fridays and had to call in to the state to tell them that I was looking for new work, new opportunities. Something in HR. I knew just what to say. I hadn't had a vacation in 16 months at FastTrak. But now I was going to take one and for as long as I could.

The first thing I was going to do was take up smoking. It was going to hurt the running, but help my attempts of getting into the Twin Palms. Getting in with Lev. The cabbies were already trading in their heavy leather jackets for simple Members Only jackets in dreary grays and blacks. They smoked Marlboro Reds. *Amerykanskie papierosy.*

In Poland, men smoked Marlboro, L&M, Golden American, Slims, Vogue, West, Pall Mall, and Rothmans. They all sounded Western and romantic to me. Golden Americans. I wish we had Golden Americans in America, mostly unfiltered and always smoked in quick succession.

I was going to be a casual smoker, I decided. I hadn't seen the women in front of the Twin Palms repeatedly snuffing out cigarettes like the men. They smoked slim cigarettes, like small straws. Virginia Slims. A few puffs finished them off.

I was going to have to invest in Virginia Slims.

I went to the convenience store and stood at the counter, scanned the cigarettes and asked to see several packs. I wanted to see how slim they were. There were Virginia Slim Luxury Light 120s, Ultra-Light 100s, Ultra-Light Super Slim 100s, and Ultra-Light 120s. I wanted to know which one was the slimmest. Which cigarette would look like a thin coffee straw between my fingers. Which version would make me look dainty and nimble-fingered. The clerk couldn't help me so I bought them all and I opened them on the street. I opened each pack and pulled out each slender stick. I crushed several between my fingers by accident. Creases formed along the stem of the Ultra-Light Super Slim 100s as I tried to perch it in between my index and middle finger. It wasn't working. My fingers weren't thin enough. The elongated straws made my fingers look like sausages. Over-plump sausages. I didn't look sexy at all. I would have to take them home and practice.

I sat on my balcony on my dining chair and dropped extin-guished Virginia Slims into the overflowing ashtray at my bare feet. The Slim Luxury Light 120s seemed to be the best fit for my fingers. Their length and luxury looked best crooked in my hand. I inhaled deeply and saw Lev approaching. I smiled as I exhaled slowly. Allowing the smoke to luxuriate between my lips like it was supposed to. He came up and stared at my feet. At the white, crushed pile.

"Have you been here all night?"

I stared up at the sky becoming brighter. Morning, finally. Then down at my feet at the wrappers from my Virginia Slims purchase escaping the black convenience bag. "No, just a little while."

He stared at me. I kept inhaling and exhaling.

"You smoke those old Russian women cigarettes."

I snubbed out the 120 into the pile of others and stared at them. I couldn't look at him.

"Hello?"

I finally looked up, sick from the Slims. "It's something new."

"I see you running. You shouldn't smoke." He played with the dry leaves on my ficus plant. Tugging at them. "I see Polish girls smoking and they don't look good when they're older."

He scolded me like a father would. I didn't want to think of him as a father. As my father, or as anyone's father.

"Or do what you want," he said.

I pushed the rest of the packs in the black plastic bag with my foot, under my chair. He pulled the leaves off the tree and dropped them on the concrete sidewalk, in front of me and in front of my balcony. Cluttering the walkway.

"I'll probably quit soon." I tried to make it sound convincing. Like it was a decision I'd been laboring over, losing sleep over.

"I'll see you around, Anka."

He started walking away, pulling out a cigarette from his pack and lighting it. He called me *Anka*. The diminutive, the child tense. He didn't take me seriously.

He turned around and inhaled deeply, squeezing his eyes like he was in pain or trying to smile. He kept staring at me while walking away.

"HEY." LEV WAS STARING AT ME THROUGH THE

screen. He was watching me walk around my apartment with my towel slipping off. "Aaaanka."

He sang it to me. "Aaaanka. Aaaanka. Aaanka."

The rest was in Russian and I couldn't understand. He was smoking outside my window. Calling to me like a tomcat. I pulled my towel up and tight.

He was speaking in Russian. Singing in Russian. I could only understand "Anka." He smiled at me. "Anka, come here."

I went toward the screen. Unsure. "What are you doing?"

"Come out here," he slurred, accent thick. He looked at me, lids hanging low over his eyes.

He wanted to come inside, come home with me, instead of one of the Russian women at the Twin Palms. Or he wanted to push me up against his car. Like the other men did. Like how I saw them do it.

"Anka..."

The rest was a slur of Russian.

He was singing it to me.

"You'll wake up the neighborhood."

"*Lyubimaya moya... Laskovaya moya... Devochka moya*, Anka..."

The last one stopped me. Little girl. *Devochka*. Little girl. My little girl. Anka.

He was smiling at me. Beckoning to me and humming to himself. "Come here, *devochka.*"

I finally slid out of the screen door. Onto the balcony. Only a concrete divider between us.

"*Devochka moya.*" He pulled me close and I could smell his breath. The hot, boozy breath on my cheek. I pulled away. Away from his tattooed fingers and backed into my apartment.

"*Devochka,* where are you going?" His breath reached me through the screen. He pleaded with me to come back.

"Not tonight." I closed the door. And let him moan away. Singing my name and lacing it with Russian. I pulled my towel tighter and turned off the light. I stood in the darkness and watched him watch me. He couldn't see me anymore but he could sense me there. He sang my name and sang *devochka* over and over and over again. He stared at me with his shark eyes. Lights turned on and flooded over Lev and he looked upstairs, blinking. He stared up and the lights turned off. Nothing was yelled down from the Ukrainian, for the first time.

I watched him withdraw like an animal and I wasn't scared.

He was drunk like the men from the villages in Poland. Carousing. Knocking on doors and waking us up in the middle of the night. Looking for their women. Or other women. Anyone warm. I wanted to feel hot, boozy breath on my cheek. I wanted it to wake me up. Back then, I wanted to feel their drunken fingers fumbling at me. I wanted to hear them whisper me awake and tell me to open my legs. I wondered what it would be like in the village, when the men came home from the bar. I wondered if I would make a good village wife, or if I would talk back too much, if I would let them fumble. I would. I would pretend to be asleep when they got home. I'd hear the stumbling and I'd keep my eyes closed, hear the water go on, hear them washing up for me, the footsteps coming closer. I would wait, pretending to sleep. I would make a good Polish wife. I would lie still.

I wondered if Lev would mind if I was still or if he'd want me to act like I liked it. I wanted to know if it was different with a Russian man. If they felt like I did. I wanted to know how close they were to us and if it was just a question of proximity.

I thought about all of this as I lay in my bed, listening to the birds sing outside my window trying to mate with one another under the nighttime heavy orange lights.

THERE WERE CIGARETTE BUTTS ON THE SIDE-

walk outside my doorway in the morning. I picked one up.

Marlboros.

I figured they were Lev's but they could have been from the hostel on the corner. The students had begun to trickle in. Europeans on holiday. The girls passed my door. Teenagers with backpacks. I started to get jealous thinking of Lev looking at the young girls in shorts and snug tank tops and I would glare at them as they passed, as they tried to find their way up and down and through the grid. I hoped they would get lost. Lose their way back to the hostel. End up in Inglewood or worse yet, Palms. My neighbor in the *chustka* had already started sweeping the sidewalk for the morning. Her *chustka* had mirrored circles dangling from the fringe and she was edging toward me. I saw her staring at the pile littered around my feet and each tug of the brush across the pavement brought her closer. She wanted to clean up. Make sure no one saw them. She wouldn't look at me and I could only think that she wanted me to forget about them too. She stared down, tugged and pulled, back and forth across the pavement and said something to me in her language. She didn't smile and she wouldn't make eye contact. She just muttered and droned. I let her sweep away the evidence as Lev walked up. She picked up her broom and disappeared back into her apartment.

"*Pree-vet, kra-sa-vee-tsa.*" That's how he said it.

"What?" I stared at him blankly.

"You don't know Russian at all?" He kicked at a butt on the sidewalk.

"What'd you say?"

"Doesn't matter."

"*Pree-vet.*"

"Just means hello. Don't worry about it."

I leaned down and started picking at snubbed out cigarettes that my neighbor had missed.

"What are you doing?"

"Cleaning up your mess."

He stepped back. He wore thick black sunglasses and I could see the crow's feet around his eyes. It was early for him. I hadn't expected him yet. "What mess? I don't see mess."

I pointed to the doorway where my aging neighbor had disappeared.

"If you'd let me in there'd be no mess out here."

"You were drunk."

"You never seen man drunk before? *Fignjá.*"

He was calling bullshit.

I stood up and stared at him. Gathered the half-smoked, crushed cigarettes in my hand and started walking away from him.

"You were walking in front of the window. Nearly naked. What could I do?"

I don't know why but looking at him – his face swollen and ruddy – I wanted him to work harder.

He should have begged.

I didn't answer him and just kept walking. Toward the alley and toward the dumpster. He followed me, close. I could hear his steps, his attempt to get in line with mine. He was following me to the dumpster. I crossed pavement and dumped the cigarette butts in the bin, turned on my heel and stared at him.

"All that for a few cigarettes?" he said.

I had embarrassed myself by being overly dramatic.

"You American girls are all the same." He started walking away.

"Like what?"

"*Zanudi.*"

I searched for a Polish translation. Something similar.

Zanudzać.

Nudzić.

It all meant the same.

Boring.

"Speak English," I said.

I wanted to pretend I didn't know what he said. I wanted to hear him say it to me again. He turned around and took off his sunglasses and looked at me cold with his pocket eyes. He wanted to make sure I saw him, his face and his eyes. And then he turned away, walked out of the alley and back to the Twin Palms.

I watched him walk and he didn't turn around this time. He didn't check to see if I was watching him. He just knew. I contemplated chasing him. But he had called me an American. Common.

"*Spierdalaj!*"

It was all I knew. He turned around, laughing. "The mouth you have."

I smiled at him.

"Didn't your mother teach you better?"

I shook my head no, coyly.

"Come here, Anya."

I walked real slow. Counted each step. I made him wait.

When I came up to him he took off his sunglasses and he smiled at me and he didn't look so bad anymore.

"What do you do, Lev?"

"What you mean?"

"What are these?" I held up his fingers gently and we looked at the rings tattooed on.

He squeezed my hand and pulled it away. "If you were Russian I could tell you."

He winked at me.

"Lev!"

He turned around and the thin man from before was standing there. He started speaking in hurried Russian and Lev started moving, leaving me in the alley. Then he stopped and turned around and came back.

"Anya, I'll come for you tomorrow."

I nodded.

He left quickly and I began to panic.

When tomorrow? Where tomorrow? I stood in the alley for a long time. Hoping he would come back and tell me that it wasn't going to happen. He was rushed. He wasn't thinking. I wouldn't have to go through anything. Why did I nod? I was ill prepared for any kind of evening with him. A truck rolled by with a flat bed full of broken down cardboard boxes. They stared at me, slowed and whistled, then said something in Spanish, whistled. I scowled and began to move. I would have to prepare. I would have to start with my undergarments.

I remember the first time I saw my grandmother's bra hanging in the shower in her apartment. It was large and sturdy. It was peach colored or off-white or maybe just discolored. One side was slapped over the top of the bar and the other hung down, limp and dripping. I touched it, pressed in the fabric. It was thick, synthetic feeling. Like it was made from something that was supposed to pass for satin. The cups were terrifyingly huge. I had hoped that I would never fill in like that. She was "full figured." She had blossomed early. I would have to enhance my blossoming.

I was going to get a bra today, but Miracle Bras were too expensive. I would have to go for the imitations. The imitations didn't have the same gel-like quality to them. The firmness and "realness." The pads of the cheap ones were stiff, curved, but only $14.99. The best I could get. I walked into the dressing room of the discount store and saw the sallow faces of the red-shirted women sifting through the bring backs. The mountain was growing as people kept tossing the items that did not work onto the pile and walking out. I waited my turn. The woman took my bras and counted them. Took a blue placard with the number eight written in white and shoved it on the hook on the door. She tried to untangle the plastic hangers from one another as she put them in the dressing room for me. It wasn't work-ing. The straps were impossibly tangled. She gave up and tossed them onto the bench, weaved around me, and shut the door. I stared at myself in the mirror. The lighting was bright and crass. My makeup was smudged. My skin pale. I wondered if a trip to the tanning salon might not be a bad idea. I took off my shirt and bra. I still had tan lines from the previous summer. It didn't make sense but I went with it. The first bra was black and sim-ple. Too small. I thought purchasing an A cup would make me look like the girls in the Victoria Secret ads. "The cup runneth over." My breasts just flooded out on the sides and underneath my armpits. I would have to go back to my size. I was losing circulation. The room was getting hot and it was small and I was having a hard time moving my arms. I took off my pants to get a general overview of what I was working with. My ass had a flabbiness that prevented me from feeling comfortable in thong underwear. I felt too exposed, too free-flowing. I opted for a full-bottomed brief to go with the padded bra. My breasts heaved over the line of the cup of my next choice. I wondered if it was too much. I would take my chance. I slid a tank top over the cups. The fabric stretched to cover the new size, the new shape. Two melons affixed to my chest. If this didn't work I would invest in those silicone breast enhancers that cancer patients purchased. I would have to check the price on those.

I stepped out of the car and onto the street with my new swollen-looking chest, barely masked by a low-cut tank top that showed off my cavernous cleavage. The shading and shadow between the two lumps intrigued me to no end. The Ukrainian man from across the street let his eyes rest on me a while longer. The crocheted curtain moved a bit and I heard a sharp knock, his wife watching, no doubt.

He continued hosing down the bushes and turned around. Men were predictable. Breasts never failed. Round and pert were best and that is what I had now. My eyes were kohled and my bra was making my breasts supple. A lot for two in the afternoon. A lot for an audience of one aging Ukrainian man.

I needed to fix my roots next. I couldn't go back to the salon. She had ruined it anyway and if I did I would have to send a bad check to the Department of Water and Power for the month.

I purchased a box of Herbal Essences hair color. The shade was #57 – Brown, Cool and Collected. The girl on the box looked pretty and her hair looked dark. On the back of the box was a "Moxie Meter." It asked me if I had ever given a piece of my mind to my boss. Or if I had ever flirted with a policeman. It said I could do either of those things and then blame it on the color. It seemed like the right choice. I dyed my hair and then my scalp and around the roots and my forehead and I tried to scrape and bleach my skin and get the color off. I should have followed the directions and rubbed Vaseline on my forehead to protect it from the dye. But I didn't. I hoped and prayed that by tomorrow the stain, the evidence, would be gone and I would be big-busted and dark-haired and exotic again.

It was dark and late and no one was at my window. I tried to sleep but couldn't, so I listened to the birds again. They stayed up all night with me. They tangled themselves together in the ivy and they gurgled and cooed and I thought of Lev and I thought of what we would do together. I wouldn't get drunk. I would go into the Twin Palms and be on his arm. I would do that willingly. I tried to visualize the Twin Palms while I lay there. What was inside. If the waiters wore tuxedos. How big it was. If it had secret entrances. If it spilled into the other buildings. Where you stood and where you sat. What you ate.

I tried but I couldn't even imagine it.

HE NEVER CAME.

I sat there and waited for hours. I sat on the couch. I crossed my legs and uncrossed them. I tried to look as if I was engrossed in what was on television. I stood up, sat down. Stood up again and poured myself a glass of wine. Then another and then another. White. Not red. I didn't want my lips or teeth to turn black. To give the hint that I had been waiting. I checked my breath six times. I rinsed with Scope. I flossed because I thought there had been some bread stuck in between my teeth. I ate bread because I didn't want to ruin my appetite but I didn't want to be drunk. Then I had another glass.

I washed my glass to keep myself from finishing the bottle. My sponge smelled. I needed to buy a new one. I smelled my hands and they smelled stale. That smell of old food and old cellulose. I was furious with myself and went to the bathroom and washed my hands again. I rubbed lotion on them. Expensive and perfumed. I smelled them again and could still smell the sponge. I went back to the living room and opened the sliding glass door. I went back and sat down on the sofa and changed the channel. I flipped between Channel 2 and 4 and waited for the commercials to be over.

I checked my phone, realized he didn't even have my number and stared out the sliding glass door. There was no smell or sign of anyone smoking. I wondered if standing on the balcony was too obvious. I tried it anyway. I stared out onto the street. Stared into the windows across from me into the apartments. At the flat screen TVs with loud voices and wild gesticulating arms on screen. I could see right through the crochet and wondered what the purpose was, if it was purely decorative or if they thought it broke up the action inside. I contemplated purchasing curtains of my own. I took a Virginia Slim (I wasn't sure which one) that I had hidden behind the ficus tree and lit it. Trying to make a light, a signal that I was there, and waiting, but no one came. The street was empty of cars. There were no sounds coming from the Twin Palms. The party was at The Calcutta on the corner tonight. Someone was puking on the lawn. New-to-the-neighborhood kids were having a house party, red cup and blue cup type kids. I saw the crochet move to the side. I listened to the retching and went back inside. I would have to find a way to sleep. It was already 2 a.m.

When I went to lie down the room was spinning. I had gone back and finished the bottle in a hurry, brushed my teeth again, but I could still smell the stink. If he came, he'd smell it. But then, maybe he wouldn't be able to smell my breath over his. I felt it was a safe choice at the moment. Tonight the orange lights coming from the streetlights were making me restless. I bit every nail off of every finger. I chipped the red paint away. Red. Who was I fooling?

The front door buzzed.

I had just fallen asleep. My alarm clock said 4:15 a.m. and I didn't hear any singing. I didn't move. It buzzed again.

And again.

I stared at my hands. The chips in the paint looked even more garish in the orange light. I got up quickly. The Berber carpet in my apartment kept my footsteps silent and there was a gentle tapping on the door. I looked through the peephole. He was standing there, all in black. Shirt opened at two buttons, chest hair spilling out. He was combing his hair back. Trying to look presentable. I cupped my hand to my mouth and blew. It was still a little sweet, but morning breath had begun to set in. My mouth was dry. I tried to swallow, produce some saliva but it just wasn't coming. He looked toward me, at the door. It was impossible to see me as I watched him put his head down.

I could open the door and he could know it would always be okay to come to me in the middle of the night like I was his mistress, a girl to keep away. Or I could leave the door closed, go lie down, go to sleep, hope he would come back to apologize in the morning or another day or one day soon. Or never. He didn't owe me anything. He didn't even know who I was. He could stop coming to my door. He could park on another street. Another block. Somewhere where he would never have to see me again, pass me again.

I OPENED THE FRONT DOOR. BUT NOT THE

heavy mesh screen door. I stared at him through the perforations and waited. He didn't speak or try and smile.

"Let me in, Anka."

"It's 4 a.m."

"We never said when…" He gave a little smirk.

"I thought dinner."

"We can eat."

"This is the time men come over to fuck you."

I looked at him. Wanting a severe reaction. He was too tired to argue. He just backed away from the door.

"Maybe tomorrow then," he said.

He walked away from the door and lit a cigarette. Got into his car and pulled out onto Fairfax, away from me. I watched him make every step. Watched how he lit his cigarette. Head down low, hand cupped tight, one-two-three.

He seemed to have a limp. His left foot dragging in time. I watched him carefully and noted that I had never seen that limp before. What if he had been hurt? What if he needed to be consoled? I had turned him away. I had lost my chance to console. But I hadn't prepared for consoling.

I had cleaned my bedroom. Vacuumed, picked up scraps from the floor, compressed my clothing into my closet and dusted the top rim of the headboard, just in case. I walked back into my bedroom and tripped over my shoes. I fell to the ground, face pressed against my new bra. I lay there a while. Poked at the cup, felt it bounce back. I contemplated sleeping on the floor next to it. My carpet was clean now, except for my dinner outfit that I was lying on top of. I decided I might still be a little drunk and crawled back into my bed. I would just wait until tomorrow. He was hurt, that was why he didn't come when he was supposed to. Maybe he was in a fight. I didn't even let him say anything. I just attacked. I would have to work on that – being more considerate. More sensitive. I must have still been drunk to be convincing myself of such things. A 4 a.m. Girl. That was the kind of girl he wanted me to be.

I WOKE UP LATE. I DIDN'T HAVE ANYWHERE TO

go anyway. My head hurt and I had forgotten to wash my face. My eyes hurt from the caked on makeup and my skin felt slick. I went to the bathroom and took a look at myself. I thanked God that I hadn't let Lev in. I wiped the soot caked around my eye and looked at my nails. Cracked polish, chipped like skylines and worn down to nubs. They hurt and were inflamed. I poured hydrogen peroxide over each finger. They sizzled and bubbled. I didn't want to get an infection. My mouth was still dry, soft and fuzzy, I brushed and washed and even then my eyes were still bloodshot. There was still black residue in and around my eyes. I washed again.

And then I finally gave up.

I opened the sliding glass door to the balcony.

My tree was gone. Someone had stolen my tree. I closed my eyes and opened them again. Still gone. What time was it anyway? I walked back inside the house. The microwave said 2. Sometime between the hours of 4 a.m. and 2 p.m. someone had climbed over the concrete divider and picked up a 30-pound tree and had run away with it. Or walked. How could the Borises in my building allow this to happen? I stared out across the street. None of the crochet curtains were moving. It was already hot and I had missed half the day. My balcony was now bare and I had no cover from the people walking back and forth. Sweeping, walking, dogs shitting. I stared out toward The Calcutta. There were red and blue cups littering the front yard. There were Christmas lights blinking on and off on the top railing. I shook my head and sat down. I stared down to my cigarette-hiding place and saw that they were gone too.

"Fuck."

"What happened?" My neighbor with the homemade haircut was leaning into my balcony from his mother's balcony. Into my space.

"Someone stole my tree."

"Who?"

"I don't know," I said.

I kicked at the dead leaves, they had left those. They or he. I didn't know if it was a one-man job or two. A group of kids from the hostel walked by. Maybe one of them did it. I was standing right there and they didn't even try to look at me. I shook my head and walked back inside. That tree cost me 46 dollars. I watered it every other day. I watched new buds grow. I slowed down my watering when I saw the leaves turning yellow. That tree was my tree. I had cultivated it.

I HAD SCRAPED TOGETHER ENOUGH FOR A

generic brand of cigarettes. Misty Ultra Lights. There was a pastel rainbow on the cover and besides that the package was mostly dull, white, and drab. The thin plastic covering the exterior the only point of excitement. The rainbow made the cigarettes look dated. I wondered how old they were. I was also eating a slim, long sausage. A *kabanos*. I didn't care who saw me. The sausage was dry because I had left it unwrapped in the refrigerator and it tasted like jerky. I had a jar of horseradish next to me and I would dip the sausage into the jar and pull out a clump at the tip and eat it. That mixed with the cigarette I was furiously inhaling made my breath hot and sour. I leaned back in my chair and heard a creak and snap. The crack at the bottom of the chair was getting worse and I didn't care. I snuffed out the Misty and started another one. Stared at the round, empty circle on the concrete and contemplated my next move.

The Weather Channel said it was 100 degrees and the streets were empty. Hot and dry and hard to breathe. They commanded the old people to stay inside and guard small children from the sun. There was no cover for them. Two fires had broken out in the valley and they had already named them. The Moorpark and the Tierra Rejada. I liked Tierra Rejada better although some of the newscasters were having trouble saying it correctly. Ash was coming down in specks on the cars on Fairfax. The air was hot and I knew if I kept the windows open my room would begin to smell like smoke at night. It happened every year during the Santa Anas. The fires. It made everyone crazy, wild-eyed, more so than even earthquakes. I had already lived through two of those here, so one more earthquake wasn't going to do a thing.

It was too hot to walk around during the day. The sun was cruel and I was too hung over to want to sweat. When the sun went down the heat stayed. The wind blew back and forth and I wanted to see the city at its best. I walked up Fairfax. Up past the aging costume store, worn out castles painted on the side of a building, trying to depict princes and kings and jousts. It was a weak representation of medieval times and was getting torn down to build high-priced condos anyway. I didn't know how much they could get for places that had a view of Genghis Cohen and the Oki-Dog stand. They could try. I walked up Fairfax toward Sunset and watched the cars get nicer and nicer. Small rusted compact Japanese cars covered in ash became Lamborghinis and Bentleys covered in ash. Those cars had windshield wipers working furiously to get rid of the ash. Those cars were speeding back and forth trying to escape the ash. I walked down Sunset toward the up-lit billboards advertising booze and women and jeans and dresses and everything I wanted and my unemployment check could not afford me. I walked past the roads leading up into the hills and the houses slanting down the hills. The Chateau – Los Angeles's own castle, and past the fraying palm trees. They were dropping fruit and fronds all along the boulevard, down on girls holding down their dresses and plastic bags careening through the air. The ash was mixing with the fruit and the dust and burning my eyes. People were taking cover in the bar with the electric bull and mini-burger sliders. I wanted to go in but the idea of walking around with a phallic plastic Mai Tai cup with multi-colored straws made my stomach turn. I would keep on my path, keep on Sunset. I thought about walking all the way to the ocean, miles, over the 405 but gave up quickly and turned down Doheny. Tired already. Los Angeles was on fire. Lev was gone. And I had shrapnel in my eyes from the palm trees and burning hills. Well, that wasn't exactly true. The Hollywood Hills weren't on fire. Franklin and above were fine. So were Doheny Estates. It was just the valley that was on fire. But somehow the wind carried the smoke and remnants of mobile homes and cul-de-sacs and tract homes all the way here, to sit on the swimming pools of the owners of the rose bushes in the Doheny Estates. Greystone Manor adjacent.

The fires made the air ten degrees hotter. The Citibank thermometer said it was really 109 degrees. There was a faint buzzing in the air, quieter than the rumbling buses. But there I could hear it and walk toward it, toward low hanging branches, and I saw the flicks through the night. They were flying in a tornado formation. They kept me in the eye as I walked up Fairfax; past the people already lined up for a chance to get on The Price is Right. Some wore shirts that matched. Some already had The Price is Right t-shirts. They were veterans. They sat on lawn chairs, smarter than those who had simply set down jackets to sit on. One man had foam fingers and multi-colored plush hats and wild eyeglasses – owlish and round.

I couldn't concentrate on that right now. I was being surrounded by bees. Hornets or yellow-jackets. I couldn't tell. The swarm was moving too quickly. The dirt from the empty lot was being kicked up around me. I picked up speed, a clipped walk. A bee flicked into my cheek and I started to run. I tried to outpace the bees. They continued to flick against my face. One, two, three, then four flicks at once. No stings. Just kamikaze bees careening toward my face, attacking my arms. Then I felt one. A bee crawling around my bra, inside the cup. I wrestled my hand into my shirt. Down, through the v-neck opening as I pushed it aside with my palm. I stuck my hand into the cup and worked my hand down, looking for the bee. I stopped running, stooped down, jiggled my bra with both hands and tried to untangle the bee. It stung me.

"Fuck."

The bees continued their tornado down the street, back under their tree as I held the dead bee in my hand. Their comrade. His face was flat, black and yellow. I cupped him in my hands and sat down on the sidewalk. I stared down inside the cup of my bra. I had a pink bump growing on the underside of my breast. Next to stretch marks I had never noticed before. It hurt.

The wings of the bee shimmered in the orange streetlight. Not shimmered, really. Gleamed. It was dead and my breast was swelling and now I had discovered stretch marks. I threw the bee in the gutter, got up, and started walking back to the apartment.

I walked up the stairs to my door, stared at my balcony, and saw Lev sitting there.

I knew my hair was in disarray. I had ripped my hands through it in a bee fit, when I felt little wings beating against my scalp.

I wasn't ready for Lev.

"You look like shit." He smiled at me. It was his come on.

I smiled at him demurely, "Thank you."

I walked into the apartment and shut the door. I heard him knock. I opened it. I didn't care. He pushed me against the wall and he pulled my shirt up. He had the intoxicating smell, onions and cologne, and I wanted to press my face into the crevice of his armpit but I didn't.

He kissed me hard and I let him and he tugged at my hair and I let him. He kissed my breast. The swollen one. I cringed. It hurt. He bit it. I screamed. He didn't stop. When I pushed him away he fell against the couch.

"What's the matter, Anka? You don't like me?"

I smiled at him. I felt woozy, as if I had caught his intoxication. "I like you fine."

I smiled at him weakly. My shirt on the floor. The V stretched at the seams. My bra on the floor.

"Why don't you come sit on the couch, on my lap?" He sat down and patted his lap.

I stared down at my swelling breast and thought about his offer. I walked over slowly. He was already undoing his belt, then the button, then the zipper. Untucking his shirt. Pulling the ends out from his waistband. Unbuttoning each button hurriedly and pulling it away from his undershirt. The armpits were stained yellow. He didn't notice but I couldn't help but stare. He pawed at me. Pulled at me. Made my choice for me.

"Stop acting, Anka."

He pulled me on top of him and he pulled at my hair, let the rest of the tendrils loose.

I pulled my head back, in motion with his tug.

He liked that.

I could tell.

He leaned in close to my breasts. Kissed at them. He saw the swelling. Touched it.

"What happened, *devochka?*"

"Bee sting."

He kissed it gently. Let go of my hair. Tried to be tender. It was nice and I liked it and I knew I shouldn't be letting him do what he was doing. He didn't deserve me but it felt nice and I wasn't going to make him stop. He pulled me into my room and took my clothes off and for once I was able to drown out the sound of the birds outside.

When we finished he rolled over and wouldn't look at me. I stared at his back. It was fleshy and white and reminded me of the underside of a whale. He had faint stretch marks above his ass and his ass was hairy. He wasn't turning around and I had to focus on something. There were a few pimples as well. I began to wonder if I had pimples on my ass too. I could hear him snoring lightly and felt that our fucking didn't warrant a nap. It wasn't hours. Or even half an hour. It was more like 20 minutes. The kind of sex where you hurriedly put your underwear back on... made sure you were posing so that the dimples on the side of your thigh were not visible and your breasts looked high and perky, not flat like pancakes. But he wasn't behaving like that. He wasn't tugging on his underwear. He wasn't looking at me. He was asleep in my bed and I wondered how long he would stay there. I didn't have the right to touch his back or get in close to him or coax him into letting me into his arms. We were strangers. I wanted a Misty Ultra Light bad, or maybe just a 120. I was scared to get up and wake him. I figured he was immovable and he was taking up so much of the mattress that I wouldn't be able to get any sleep anyway. I started to get up. Inch by inch I moved my legs away from him. He didn't move, he didn't heave, he didn't even notice.

I got up quickly and ran from the guttural growls and from his smell. I went onto the balcony and hunted around for stray cigarettes. One I had dropped, somewhere. I found a half. It was mostly submerged in soot-colored water. I weighed my options. There were really only two. Yes or No. I hunched down and picked it up. I pulled off the wet part, left a little nub and struck a match. It would have to do. It fizzled when I tried to light it. I pulled a little more off; the tobacco flaked and stuck to my wet fingers. The flakes transferred onto the stem of the Slim as I tugged at it and re-lit it. Inhaled deeply.

One and a half drags was all that Misty Ultra Thin could give me. I had fucked him. Now what? I wanted to get into the Twin Palms. I wanted to be more than just his Fairfax girl. I wanted to be his main girl. The only girl. Men like him didn't have just one. I had to stand out from all the others. I had to make myself more tantalizing. I wanted his soft white underbelly over me nightly. Groaning and sweating and cursing me while he thrusted. He never used the word *suka* for me so I figured I was okay. He didn't know that I knew what it meant. He didn't know anything about me.

I came back into the room and he was letting out whimpers now. I decided to rouse him. I touched his back, it was warm and clammy. He didn't move. I walked around and stared at his front. His belly obscured most of his penis. There was only some on display. He looked like a small child, overwrought and over-nourished. His hands were covered in those rings. Black marked and chubby. I touched one of them. They were rough. Like a worker's hand. I was surprised. I thought he would have soft child's hands. Why hadn't I noticed when he was running his hands over me? Because he wasn't. He was tugging and pawing. He had moved his hands quickly, efficiently. When I touched his hand he made a sound. Murmured something in Russian that I didn't understand. So I touched it again and he opened his eyes and said, "What is it?"

I wanted him to fuck me again but I didn't know how to ask so I backed away and let him close his eyes and waited for the sleep sounds to start up again. They finally did and I left the room. I walked from the bathroom to the kitchen to the living room, sat on the couch, waited, got up, waited, stood in the dining room and stared at the smeared fingerprints on the glass table and started to clean. The sofa was pushed in 6 inches on one side. The remnants of the previous night looked almost violent. But it wasn't violent. It was nearly boring, ordinary sex, but still better than nothing.

NOW HE WASN'T MOVING, JUST TAKING UP MY

bed. I tried to move the couch silently. When being silent I usually made the most noise. The sofa creaked and squealed as I moved it 6 inches back into position. I waited to hear something, but just heard the sounds of sleep. Was it impolite to ask him to leave?

I should have told him I didn't like sleeping next to people. I should have told him I had to get up early. But he knew I didn't.

There was a knock at the door. I checked myself in the mirror to make sure I looked like I hadn't just gotten fucked or maybe to make sure that I did.

"I have another fish." My neighbor was standing there, his mustache more trimmed on one side than the other. His glasses were smeared and I had the urge to clean them with my table cleaner.

"Really?"

"Mackerel." He held up the bloody package. He smiled and waited for my impression of this fact.

"Excellent."

"I will gut one for you."

"No, no."

"And smoke it. You love smoke. I see it."

"I don't really like smoked fish."

"It's what we do. It's what we eat."

It was of no use. He wasn't listening.

"I bring tomorrow."

He walked away smiling and I shut the door. The conversation of the smoked fish had woke up Lev, who was scratching himself and stretching in the doorway of my bedroom.

"Who was that?"

"My neighbor, next door."

"*Derevenshina.*" He spit the word out and turned back to the bedroom.

"What's that?" I followed him. He wasn't waiting. He wasn't getting ready to fuck me again. He was putting his socks on. Looking for his underwear. His pants.

"Peasant."

"Where are you going?" I asked.

All of a sudden I didn't want him to go. I wasn't sure what I wanted from him, not to leave yet, for sure.

"I have things to do." He wouldn't look at me as he said it. I knew he didn't like being asked. I wanted to ask him again. I wanted to own him. I wanted to let him own me. He got dressed and moved past me quickly. Told me he'd see me around.

He didn't say it like that.

He said, "I'll see you."

Not around. Not later. Not soon.

When he left I went back into my room and I stared at my sheets. One corner had pulled away from the mattress. On his side. It had crumpled beneath him and stayed like that while he creased it and sweat on it. My sheets were floral. Decidedly childish. Laura Ashley. My mother sent them to me the first time I lost my job. She felt a new set of sheets would be a fresh start. The old ones had roses that were too big and the navy backdrop was supposed to cause anxiety dreams. That's what *Cosmopolitan* magazine said. The anxiety my bed sheets were causing me in my sleep were causing me to be late to work which caused me to be fired. But now, these sheets were worn through. The middle faded, the rubber band threaded around the frame of it was loose, causing just this kind of pull to happen and exposing my cheap mattress. I hoped he hadn't noticed.

I fixed the sheets. They were still damp on his side. They felt sticky and I didn't want to be in them anymore. Dried sweat layered with new sweat. His smell. I inhaled deeply. It started making me sick. I kept inhaling anyway. Till the nausea came. I got up and ran to the bathroom. Kneeled in front of the toilet and waited for it to come up and when I saw that he had left a ring of shit in my toilet… it did.

Afterward, I decided that washing the sheets would be the best idea. I pulled them off. I put them in a pile in my room and turned on the ceiling fan and turned it on full blast. I waited for the smell to rush out of the windows and into the alley. It didn't. It clung to the mattress where he laid and labored. It clung to the mattress. It clung to the walls.

I tried my first attempt at leaving then.

THE LITTLE LIMB OF THE GAS GAUGE SAID MY

car had six gallons of gas in it. My rent was due in two days. My check from the government was already in the mail. It would probably come on the third day. I could hold everything off until then. If I took the 405 Freeway I would sit in traffic for hours and my car would overheat and I would be down to two gallons of gas. Minimum. It was 3 p.m. I pulled some clothes together. I had to rush. I left the sheets in the washer of my building. I didn't have enough quarters for the dryer. Someone, maybe the fish man, would take pity on me. More likely I'd find them in a pile on the floor on the concrete, mildewy and dank, but I didn't care.

I drove down Sunset Boulevard, through the winding of billboards. My favorite part was coming up. The Chateau Marmont was looming over the boulevard looking French. It negated the advertisements for slim jeans and elaborately rhinestoned popstar fragrances and made things look stately.

The cars weren't snaking back and forth yet. Heading back to their apartments from Century City assistant jobs and executive jobs and movie lot jobs. I knew this because I had placed temp candidates for them and I knew where the hot jobs were. Century City. Near Cheviot Hills and Beverlywood and Rancho Park and everything that sounded nice.

I kept driving through Bel Air. Stared at the gates, took the turns quickly on Sunset, where I always pretended to be a race car driver, past the Jacaranda trees, and pulled alongside the 405 and saw the jam. In both directions, the cars were slowly stalling and stuck. Traffic had started early so I would have to continue further.

When I came to the mouth of Sunset the ocean was in front of me. I pulled right onto PCH and drove alongside the water. The sun had burned through the fog. The sky looked endless and the houses were pouring down all around me. I pulled over and crawled down a dirt cliff onto the sand.

I sat on the beach and stared at the expanse of sky. The waves crashed down and the water wanting to smother me. The sun was too much so I wandered into an embankment next to a house. I hoped they weren't home and wouldn't come after me. The sheen on the water was making me sick, making my eyes hurt. I closed them but the flicker was still there. I touched my hands to my face and his smell was still on me. It smelled like dried saliva, it was sour and I didn't want it on me anymore. If I went to the water I would throw up in it. I went down and sat in the embankment and covered my hands in the cool, damp sand hoping the salt would take away the smell and closed my eyes. I rubbed them deep in the sand in a frenzy, purposely taking off layers of my skin.

I rubbed them raw and then I fell asleep.

"Get up and get out."

I opened one eye at a time. A middle-aged man in yellow swim trunks was kicking at me. He had gray chest hair rolling down his chest in white ripples. He saw me staring and got self-conscious. He stopped kicking, then collected himself and started nudging me with his toe.

"Stop kicking me."

"Get up then."

"Jesus, give me a second."

I was slow to get up. He kept his foot near me and I swatted at it.

"Get out of here," I said.

That made him incredulous. "I live here. You get out!"

"Goddamnit." I tried getting up. My hands were caked with sand. I started rubbing off the sand and moaned. Remembering what I had done. My hands were pink like dead baby skin. Abrasions in between my fingers. On the prints.

"What'd you do to yourself?" He was staring at my hands as I was staring at his chest hair. Layers were falling on top of layers on top of his nipples. I hadn't even reached his face yet. The fuzz covered his shoulders too. He was like a great big polar bear in yellow swim trunks. He started nudging me with his toe again.

"Do that again and I'll break your toe." I couldn't swat at him this time. My hands were throbbing.

"You think you're tough? Get up."

I did what I was told but I didn't like it. "I need a cigarette."

"It's fire season."

I tried to stand up without using my hands. It was tough.

"What did you do to your hands?"

"None of your business. Do you have a cigarette or not?"

"No, I don't."

It was no use. I walked away from him and the beach. I didn't want to feel nauseated anymore anyway. I turned toward the water one more time and stared real hard. It trembled under the weight of the shine and then it crashed into the sand.

Driving was a bitch. That fur ball man was right. What had I done? I had two skinned baby rabbits for hands and I was having trouble keeping them out of the sun. I put the visor down but that only obscured my vision driving down PCH. I needed salvation. Or Vaseline. Something. I pulled into the parking lot of CVS and walked in, holding my hands down. I found Vaseline. I slathered it on in the car. The sand that was still stuck scraped deeper and deeper and mixed with the yellowish jelly and created a thick coat over my fingers. I clung to the steering wheel and sat in the traffic snaking down and around the glittering ocean.

IF THAT HAD TAUGHT ME ANYTHING AT ALL IT

was that I should never leave the house again. My sheets were gone. Not even in a heap on the concrete floor in the laundry room. One of the Russians had stolen them and put them on their own beds, no doubt. I thought about all the men who had been with me on those sheets. Not many, really.

Each one put his head on the pillowcase. Or pushed my face down into the pillowcase. We had all thrashed around between the same duvet and full-fitted sheet.

All but one.

I lay down on my bare mattress and watched the ceiling fan rotate. I held my Vaseline hands up to cool down, to stop the throbbing. His smell was still here. In the mattress. I felt it in my skin again. Old, turned milk. All men have that smell. It stays on the skin, settles in between the follicles. I kept smelling my arm, both arms. Repulsed and intoxicated. I wanted to erase him and keep him. What did I smell like on him? Was he smelling his hands as he drove? Did he try to erase me too?

THE FIRST TIME I SMELLED THE TURNED MILK

smell was in Poland. The tenements were fading and crumbling. The walls were stained with soot from passing Fiats and Volkswagens. The wallpaper in our apartment in Poland had yellowed. The plastic floral tablecloth had stayed the same, faded in new places. Food smells from the neighbors tumbled through the walls. Chicken fat from soup and dried sausages mixed with urine from the pipes in the bathroom. It accumulated from each bathroom and ran down the pipes in the apartment. The smells seeped into the beds, the sofa, and the carpet. I would hold my face down and inhale through my mouth. Inhale until I felt like bursting, and then hold my face up and gasp for air. My mother would open the windows and curse the neighbors. Curse the chicken fat smell. The smell was heavy in the air coming through the windows and from above. We couldn't escape it.

I watched out the window as the starlings pulsed back and forth. Over the trees, TV antennas, and big gray *bloki*. They swirled over the park, once an old Jewish cemetery that the Communists tore through, ransacked the headstones and built walkways and planted trees. My mother used to walk us there, daily. There were no signs of headstones anymore. Everything wiped away. Only the birds kept watch. Swirling above and congregating in the trees. They didn't fly anywhere else in the city.

Just here. Over the *bloki*, through the sky, over the old cemetery, and over the park.

In Poland, they do three kisses. Once per cheek and then another one. An extra one – the one that tripped me up. One cheek, next cheek, back to the first cheek. There was Polish. They spoke so fast and I tried to understand between the giggles. I stared and smiled and looked coy and they told me how pretty I looked and I smiled even more and then he came and he kissed me and I was confused and I kissed one cheek, another cheek, and then panicked and we both went for the mouth and then I switched to the cheek again and his wife and everyone around us laughed. He smiled and patted my back and I didn't even know who he was. They set up a long table in their apartment and no one could move around it. The tablecloth was sticky and plastic and covered in burnt orange flowers and brown stems. Strictly Eastern Bloc fare. The *galaretka* of chicken pieces, carrots, and peas suspended in a yellow gelatin were served in dainty coffee cups with curved handles, and sat among bowls of cucumbers in sour cream and dill, pickle soup, tripe soup, borscht, *gołąbki*, potatoes with dill, *bigos* (hunter's stew), kielbasa steaming and split open.

My plate was layered with food. Crowded in by it. Cherry cordial. Homemade wine from the village. *Sharlotka* for dessert. I ate everything. Swallowed the pickle soup, watched the sour cream separate and rise to the top, swelling and clouding in the bowl. I caught him staring once or twice. My one-armed auntie caught it too. She made the dinner all by herself. She circled the table and watched us eat. Listened to us slurp.

My mother had stopped making pickle soup long ago and she did not know how to make *sharlotka*.

They wanted to hear about America.

We used to send them blue jeans when we couldn't get back into the country, before the Communists left in 1991.

Wranglers, Levis, sometimes Guess. They would send letters begging for blue jeans and my mother put together boxes for them. Everything American. Even things we didn't have. Behind their backs she would call them vultures. When we came they were wearing our blue jeans. He was staring at me and he was wearing blue jeans my mother bought him. A 34-inch inseam. I remember. When he stared at me my face got hot. When he spoke to me I didn't understand him. He asked about school and friends and I smiled and nodded. Yes. I had both. I averted my eyes and stared at the curtains. Billowing and lacy and yellowing. The adults were talking. Talking about who had died. Who had cancer. Who was next.

He asked me if I wanted to go see the *dzialka* behind the apartments. My mother pushed me out of my chair. She said yes for me, that I did want to see the garden. She told me to stop looking so bored, in English. They all smiled and couldn't understand.

We climbed down the stairs of the apartment building. Crumbly, different from our *blok*. This was a town outside the city and the buildings were squat with red doors and barns nearby. There were cows walking around and Fiats broken down beside the buildings. We walked behind the apartments and there were the gardens each family had. They were fenced in with beets, cucumbers, and tomatoes growing untended. I could hear him breathing beside me. He stuttered a few words in English and said he was taking classes. He was wearing a sweater even though it was warm out. He walked me in between the rusting chicken wire, took me where no one could see, and I wanted to kiss him. I watched his mouth moving and I thought about it.

He stared at me and said, "You like here?"

"Here in Poland? Or here in the *dzialki*?" I said.

He smiled. Laughed. "I guess both."

My back had started to sweat. Drips of sweat pooled at the waist of my pants. How could he be wearing a sweater? I gave him a coy little smile, like I thought you were supposed to do and then I turned away and picked a tomato to play hard to get.

"That's not our *pomidor.*"

He took it out of my hand and I smelled my fingers. The sour smell. The little hairs on the vines pulling away and covering my fingers as I pressed.

"Come over here."

I followed through morning glories closed and fading and scraped past the chicken wire. Closer to the line of trees and further away from the apartment. I didn't want to look at him but when I did I saw his eyes and I knew we were going to go deeper into the plots and why and I didn't turn away and I didn't go back. No one else was willing to do this for me.

He put his tongue into my mouth and I could taste the pickle soup all over again and I could taste that he had eaten herring. Even though I had been careful to avoid it.

I WENT TO BINGO BUT IT HAD BEEN CANCELED

without anyone telling me. I walked to my car, pissed about losing the $50 for the night. The cold, dry air made my hands sting. I had to walk uphill and realized I could walk a couple of blocks and see the lights of the city. Probably see my apartment from here. The lights of the Twin Palms. All of it was obscured by the lights of Hollywood Boulevard. I liked driving down Hollywood. On the east edge, near the border of Little Armenia and next to the old apartments. Some had spires. There were castles on Hayworth too, where I lived, but these were bigger, more foreboding. They weren't like the two-story stuccos built in the '70s with the tropically deceptive names. The buildings shot up and past the palm trees that lined the streets here. I drove past the Hollywood Downtowner motel and wondered what was going on in the rooms. I decided to pull into the parking lot. I opened the latched little gate and stared at the swimming pool that was up lit in the midst of the split-level stucco building. I sat down on a green plastic lawn chair and stared at the water quietly, waiting to hear sex sounds. The motel office was well lit and displayed signage stating that the establishment accepted AAA. Famous people headshots covered the walls, enticing tourists into believing that they too could see someone famous. They could sit and breathe famous air.

The air here was mild but not famous. The Santa Anas were

gone and now that thin layer of mist was covering things. Cheap geraniums were latched onto the metal fence surrounding the walkway above me. No sex sounds were starting. I tried to be extra quiet and looked at the pool. The water was still and there was a film over it. Small bugs and debris. Maybe other things mixed in. Sex things. The ladies had made me think about sex and how I would need it forever. How I'd never be able to escape it.

I got back into my car and headed home. I wanted to see Lev tonight. I wanted him and his smell. I drove down Hollywood under the 101 and down Vine, before hitting the Walk of Fame and watching tourists stop and shoot pictures of their feet on gum-covered stars.

When I pulled up to my apartment I was hoping he'd be sitting on the steps. Instead, there was a smoked mackerel wrapped in paper. I brought it inside but it made the apartment smell like an immigrant's house. I didn't know what to do with it so I put it in the refrigerator and went to take a bath.

I came out of the bathroom and I could smell the mackerel coming out of the refrigerator. It was seeping into the air and I knew by morning that it would be in the couch cushions, my chairs, and my bed. I locked myself in my room to try and get away from the smell and turned on the ceiling fan. At the highest speed the fan looked like it was going to launch off the ceiling and spin around the room, slicing and dicing. I always put it on the highest speed, hoping one day something exciting would happen.

My mattress was still barren. My unemployment check would come in a week but I hadn't allocated any funds for new sheets. I needed to burn the mackerel smell out of the apartment.

The convenience store with the big glowing ATM sign was

closed so I had no choice but to go to the magazine stand on the corner of Fairfax and Rosewood. The man selling the magazines had sparrows tattooed on his neck and he was always strung out. He had a dog with him again. It had fur missing from his face and one eye was blue and the other was brown and it just sat there and glared at me like I did something to it. So this time I was smart. I brought dry Polish sausage and fed some to the beast while the man got my cigarettes for me.

I watched people zoom around and around looking for parking spaces, make U-turns, rub their bumpers against the cars in front and behind theirs as they tried to parallel park. People were getting out, congregating in front of the Silent Movie Theater. They had well-manicured haircuts and pegged pants. They didn't live around here. The windows in the neighborhood stayed dark and uninviting, only alive during the day.

"Marlboro Lights, please." I didn't want anything fancy today. He grunted at me and leaned to get the pack. "Hard pack."

I tossed the sausage to the dog. He ate it up without question while I perused the magazines. The lights from the magazine stand were bright. Bug-killer bright. I was all alone with the dog. The man with the sparrows on his neck scratched at his arm like there was something under his skin. He was really getting in there, really looking where he was scratching. The dog took a seat next to me and waited for more sausage. It wasn't happening, but the dog didn't get it so he just kept waiting.

"Are you going to pay for these?" The man was still scratching, breaking open the skin and letting the blood pool.

"In a minute," I said.

"You're going to crease the pages."

I stared down at the magazine, holding it so I didn't give my still-pink hands any papercuts. "I'm being careful."

He looked at me, then at his dog at my leg. "Do you want a smoke?"

"I'll pay for them in a second." I purposely ripped the front page as I pushed it back in the rack.

I didn't even put it back where it was supposed to go.

"No, I mean, I'll give you one of mine."

I walked over. He was opening a pack behind him. Newport Lights. I scowled.

"What's your problem?" he asked me.

"Those have fiberglass in them."

"That's a *myth*." He spent extra time saying *myth*. "I work at a cigarette stand. I should know what's what," he said.

"You work at a magazine stand. It just happens to sell cigarettes."

He pulled back the cigarette he was offering me and looked at me like I smelled like shit. "No need to be a bitch."

I shook my head. It was either apologize or walk back to my apartment empty-handed. "I'm sorry. You definitely should know what you're talking about."

"Thank you," he said.

He shoved the Newport Light toward me and lit. "I see you here sometimes."

I wasn't listening to him. I was staring at people walking in and out of Canter's. I was salivating thinking about their carrot cake. Their cheesecake with the strawberries on it. The strawberries always looked stiff, always safely enrobed in red gelatin. The bear claws, the rugelach, poppy seed cake, black-and-white cookies, apple turnovers, cherry turnovers, five kinds of cheesecake, latticed cream cakes, *sharlotka*. Like my grandmother makes. I wanted to have one of each.

"How much are those cigarettes?"

"Eight dollars," he said.

That's a pound of carrot cake, I calculated.

"I'll come back for these."

I looked both ways and crossed Fairfax into the beaming spaceship of Canter's. On the right were pickles in brine and gravlox and layers of cream cheese in tins that looked like marshmallow whip. And pickled herring.

To the left was what I wanted. The smell of yeast was overwhelming. The carrot cake came in loaves, white cream cheese frosting in tufts on top.

"Whatever I can get of that for eight dollars," I said.

The man behind the counter with the heavy black mustache pulled it out of the case, cut it, weighed it, made a face, put it in a pink box, wrapped it with string, and gave me a ticket. It said $8. I had to pay the woman stooped in the cubbyhole of a seat near the bakery counter. She had a sweater clipped around her shoulders and she was using a calculator and she was writing down the amount of each ticket and then she took mine and I got my carrot cake in its pink box and I was out of there.

The carrot cake had large pieces of walnuts. That's why I liked it. The crunch. It was salty against the sweet of the frosting, so good that it made me want to cry. I ate it all, one mouthful after another like someone was going to take it away from me, as I sat and watched the fires on television.

They were coming closer. The acrid smell was faint, but already hitting this part of the city although the fires were still smoldering on the outskirts of the grid. The valley fires were moving to Angeles Crest. They said it might be a marijuana farm in the National Park. They said that they would probably never find out who did it.

I shoveled the cake in my mouth and watched the reporter on TV with a yellow rain slicker talk to the people in the studio.

"There's ash positively everywhere, Chuck. Blinding."

She was right. It was coming down all around her like snow. It was getting stuck in her hair, her lip-gloss. As she tried to free herself from it all they cut away to a commercial. When I stuck my head out the sliding glass door I could smell the smoke and the sky was a deep orange. Nuclear-style. I looked down at the cake and saw that it was gone. Just the outline of the frosting, like crime scene paint. I had to leave the house; I was feeling sick and anxious. I got into the car and started to drive east, toward the 5, the way to the mountains. In Hollywood, I realized I didn't know how to get to Angeles Crest and so I pulled into the Hollywood Downtowner motel again to see if they had some local attraction maps with directions.

It was still silent at the Downtowner. The pool lights were on and there was a shell of ash on the surface of the water. It wasn't moving, just clinging. I brushed off a lawn chair and sat down and positioned myself to be facing the mountains. It was harder to breathe at the Downtowner. I hadn't anticipated the choking and I wished that I had a gas mask or one of those surgical masks. An older couple rushed down the stairs. They were both wearing surgical masks. I wanted to ask them where they had gotten them but they ran past me too quickly.

I saw them talking to the front desk attendant through the glass and the old man was waving his hands around. The woman was trying to hold them down. He wasn't having it and the attendant ran into another room and disappeared. They waited a while. Tapped on the "ring this bell for the attendant" bell. The husband started doing it over and over again. I could hear it outside, by the pool. His wife pulled him away and he dragged their suitcases out of the office and down the street. The attendant came back. He put the "ring this bell for the attendant" bell back in its place and started cleaning up the pamphlets the old man had strewn around. I walked up and into the glass room. He looked startled when I came in, like I was going to throw something at him, like I was the old man.

I walked over to the wooden case of Los Angeles attraction pamphlets and touched them all, slowly. I could feel him staring at me but he didn't say anything. There were pamphlets for the

Griffith Park Zoo, the beautiful beaches of Malibu! Las Vegas, Sea World and the San Diego Zoo, Lake Havasu, and Reno.

"Are there more Los Angeles attractions?"

"They're all there," he said.

I turned to look at him. He was trying to look extra official; he had interlocked his fingers and made his hands into a fist, smiled at me through thin lips. "There's only two about Los Angeles. The rest are about Lake Havasu."

I picked up the pamphlet. It was covered in pictures of girls in bikinis and speedboats and personal watercrafts.

"Where are you looking to go?" He was getting annoyed.

"Angeles Crest."

"It's on fire."

"Well, I know."

"Were you sitting by the pool earlier?"

I stared at him and tried to decide what the right answer would be. I wasn't sure so I kept silent.

"I think you were. Are you a guest here?"

"No."

"What were you doing out there, then?"

"The pool looked nice."

"It's covered in ash," he said.

"Maybe you should clean it." I narrowed my eyes at him and he didn't like that at all. He disappeared into a back room. Like when the old people were yelling at him. He was waiting for me to leave too, so I walked back to the pool, to my seat, and wiped the ash off again and sat down. The wind had picked up so the water was rippling and moving the ash to one side, thick like mud. The desk boy came out and took the wand to clean the pool and started skimming it over the surface. The pool lights made him look blue and dead and he wouldn't look at me. I stared at him to try and unnerve him, and finally it worked.

"I don't think you can just sit here if you aren't a guest of the motel."

He kept skimming as he talked. I didn't move. I just looked at him. The water rippled around the skimmer. He let it go and the basket of the wand floated to the bottom.

"Who says I can't?"

"The sign says so." He pointed to the red and white sign. It was yellowed with age, the face cracked and bubbling. Guests of The Hollywood Downtowner Only.

"I just want to stay a few more minutes. No one's here anyway."

He stared at me and thought about it for a moment. "I don't want to get in trouble."

"No one's here."

"My boss might call."

"So what?"

"He's going to ask me if anything's going on."

I thought for a moment. "Nothing is."

He inhaled slowly, walked back in the office and left me alone. I went back to staring at the pool, ash floating down and coating it. The gate jangled and I sighed, thought he was coming back after me. I turned and saw a man, back turned, closing the gate behind him. The back of his shirt was wet with sweat. He turned toward the pool and I thought, he's not bad, strong-looking. He didn't look at me or the pool and just headed up the stairs, to room 214 and struggled to find his keys. I wondered if he could sense me watching him, if he did, he did not turn around. Instead, he closed the door behind him and walked inside. I turned to the office and the desk clerk was watching the door too. And then me. I closed my eyes and listened to the pool water hitting the tiles. It did make a sound if you listened closely.

"Is the water cold?"

He startled me. I opened my eyes and stared at the man from room 214. He was wearing shorts. Not swim trunks, just shorts. I told him I didn't know. He put his things on a chaise lounge under a yellow and white metal umbrella covered in ash.

He was sandy-haired and brown-eyed. He didn't look like he was from anywhere, just white, and he was what my mother liked to call a mutt. Someone who had been in America so long that they were completely washed of where they came from. He was probably 1/12 of everything and nothing at all. He was American.

When asked what he was, he would probably answer something like that, American. And what was that really? A place. A thing. He took off his shirt and jumped in before I could ask him what he was. So quickly that I wasn't even sure he took off his shoes until I saw his pink feet fluttering in the light. He swam underwater for a long time, long enough for the ash to slide closed over his entry point. He kicked his legs out like frog legs and I wasn't sure he'd ever come up for air. The desk clerk stood by the window and watched him. And I considered jumping in too, swimming after him and pulling him above the water line.

He finally surfaced and I tried not to watch. The desk clerk didn't bother to hide his curiosity – this was a new alien element in our equation. The man took a big gulp of air and went back under, back and forth, back and forth. It was hypnotic and exciting to watch him disrupt the ash. He finally came out of the pool and walked to his chaise lounge, pulled the graying towel over his face and breathed deeply into it. He was so close that I could see the goosebumps raise on his skin. The air was cool and I was sure he was feeling it, wet.

"It's nice." He finally looked at me and I still thought, handsome. It made me nervous and I looked away.

"The ash is weird, huh?" He looked at me and waited for an answer.

I stared at the flakes falling down around us.

"I've never seen it like this before," I said.

"It's because it's so close."

"It is close, isn't it?"

He leaned back on the chaise lounge and sighed. "Yeah, and getting closer."

We sat there quietly and thought about it. He closed his eyes, looking impossibly exhausted.

"Your room as bad as mine?" he asked.

I faltered. "Oh, I'm not staying here."

He looked at me for a moment and then nodded, like it made sense and everything.

"I wouldn't stay here either, but I have to stay close to the fires." He sat up quickly at the word and looked around. I wanted to ask him what he meant, where he came from. How he liked the fires.

"I guess I should get some shut eye," he said.

"Where are you from?" I asked.

He said Oklahoma, a place I had never been, not even driven through.

I had gone nearly everywhere in America, but at some point had lost my resolve to see it all, and just stopped here.

He did some kind of hat tip (without a hat) and walked up to room 214 and closed the door behind him. I looked over to the desk clerk and saw he was still watching. Now just me.

I sat there for a while, legs up. Toeing at the plastic of the chair.

Later, I got up and started walking around the pool. I slid my hand up the metal banister and started walking up the steps to the row of doors. I tried one, the one the old couple had come out of. It was locked. Then, I walked to room 214 and listened quietly. Even put my ear up to the door and stood there, trying to hear moving-around sounds. Shuffling, anything. There was nothing. The door was still warm from the daytime and I pressed both palms against it. They stung, but the warmth cut through and I wanted it for myself.

I drove the other way down Hollywood Boulevard and later

onto Benton Way. I rolled down Benton surrounded by multi-family, soot-covered and bar-windowed stucco houses. I turned on Beverly Boulevard and passed Rampart and Tommy's *Original* World Famous Hamburgers. I thought about it for a moment. A chili cheese dog. I pulled into the cramped parking lot and got in line behind everyone else and stood next to the white slant-roof building. I watched them sprinkle onions on top of the chili, on top of the dog, inside the bun. They moved like clockwork and I was in awe of them. Their white uniforms and hats. It was so easy, their movement, their task. It made me want to be good at something. Have a task.

It was my turn.

I thought about it for a moment. "Chili cheese dog. No onions. Maybe some sauerkraut." I stopped and really weighed my options.

"Yes. Sauerkraut. Two. The same."

They made them. Swiftly. They were cheap. I could have stood next to everyone else at the outside counter but I didn't. Instead, I ran to my car, spread out the napkins, and stared at them both. Suddenly they were unappetizing and all I wanted was that man. *That* man. Well, I wanted to know about him. Where he came from and why the fires. It was useless, I'd never see him again. I wasn't going back right now, I didn't want to hover. I would maybe do a drive-by later, but not so soon.

I ate the hot dogs and didn't enjoy them. I thought about the heat of the door on my tender palms.

When I turned the car on and drove away from Tommy's I headed in the wrong direction and pulled down a side street to correct myself. It was an alley and it led to a small street with apartments and houses and more bars and more soot and some palm trees and a maze of stucco.

I pulled up near a taxi stand. I didn't know how I got there or how to get away. But there he was. He was standing with other men in leather dusters and silver chains, smoking and looking at the orange smoke-filled sky. He looked at me. He looked at me and then they all looked at me and he nodded his head and I kept driving and tried to find my way out of the low-slung buildings and warehouses and barred-up side of Los Angeles. It wasn't safe here. Everything was in cages here. Kept in and kept out.

I stopped in an alley. I could finally find out more about Lev. Did I want to leave or should I turn around?

He was still standing outside when I pulled up and parked a few cars away. He didn't see me and I sat watching him, air on full blast. He was on the phone, fumbling with a cigarette in his mouth and lighter in his hand. He stopped what he was doing for a moment and started yelling. I couldn't hear because of the whoosh of air but I suspected that I wouldn't be able to understand anyway. A few cabs pulled in. A young man walked up to Lev, waiting for him to get off the phone. He did, finally and slowly. I watched as the man tried to compose himself, looked around, and began talking. He looked nervous. Lev listened patiently. He was quiet for a while after the man stopped speaking. He looked like a new immigrant wearing a silk shirt with patches of sweat, tucked into his pants. Lev raised his hand and slapped him open-handed, then again and again.

My face burned hot. This act of violence made Lev look taller, bigger, and more substantial. The man walked into the cab stand and Lev followed him in. I held back for a moment and then put the car in reverse. Had he seen me watching? Did he perform for me? I hoped so.

MY APARTMENT WAS SAFE AND HAD NO CAGE

surrounding it. I ran inside and locked the doors and windows. I crawled onto my mattress and buried my face and inhaled the mattress smells. The weave was rough against my face and my hands. I needed another coat of Vaseline or maybe I needed to move on to Neosporin. A tube cost more than a jar of Vaseline. The choice was clear. I waited to asphyxiate or fall asleep.

I woke up inhaling the smell of smoke but was alive. There was a banging at the door. I ran to answer the door and it was Lev.

"Were you following me?"

"I just woke up."

"Not now, before, when I saw you."

"When?"

He knew I was lying and I wanted to be sure which encounter he meant. Did he think I saw him as he disgraced the young man?

"Open up."

I didn't like him ordering me around anymore. I did what I was told and he pushed in. He looked upset. I thought about being scared of him. If I was or wasn't. I wasn't sure.

"It smells like burning in here."

"It smells like that everywhere."

He cornered me against the wall, near my hallway door, somewhere I couldn't wiggle out of. It wasn't sexual this time.

"What do you do?" I asked.

"Cabs."

I just looked at him and before I could ask again he responded.

"My business is mine."

"I know," I said quietly.

He didn't like my back talk and I could tell from his face he wasn't used to it.

I held my hands up and he stared at their rawness.

"What's wrong with your hands?"

"Nothing."

He grabbed one of them and I winced.

"What did you do to yourself?"

I tried to pull it away but he wouldn't let me. Finally he let me loose, a little.

"It's a burn. Or something. I don't know. I'm fine."

He looked at me and brought me into the kitchen. He looked through my cabinets and took out some items. Honey, baking powder, yogurt, something I didn't even know I had, and took out a bowl, started mixing. He slowly slid the mixture over my hands and held them over the sink. Some dripped off. He didn't say a word. My hands were shaking, all of me was shaking.

He was close. The kitchen was small and I stared at his shoulders, his leather-covered shoulders and his close-cropped haircut. Gray was creeping in between the deerskin color. I wanted to nuzzle my face in his shoulder but he wasn't that kind of person to me and I didn't have the guts. He looked at me and shook his head.

"What is it?"

"From the old country."

I looked at him and smiled. He leaned in and kissed me on the neck. Quietly and softly. His breath on my neck made my skin cover in bumps, and I blushed. He turned me toward him, ass against the sink and got down on his knees and breathed against me. Goose pimples crawled up and down my legs, my thighs, and I held my arms up because I didn't know what else to do. He looked up at me and he looked so small.

"What did you do to yourself, Anka?"

"It was an accident."

He kissed my stomach and unbuttoned my jeans and then he just stayed on his knees and kissed my underwear, lightly and gently. I stared down at him, unable to put my hands down. He was a different person now.

"I want to lie down," I said and went to wash the salve off my hands. When I finished, he led me into my room and stared at the bare mattress.

"What happened here?"

"Someone stole my sheets."

He stared at me, like he pitied me and I didn't like it.

"I'll buy you new."

"I don't need new. I can get some myself."

He shook his head, looked back at the mattress as he walked out of the bedroom. He was already on the couch when I walked in. He tried to make room for me on the couch to lie down next to him and I slid down, trying to get comfortable. I had one leg on and one leg off. I twisted around and slid my hands against his chest, but nothing was working. I pressed my face against his chest and waited to fall asleep.

I opened my eyes and looked at the creases on his face, the hair on his chest, and the tattoos on his fingers. He was handsome, I thought. Not like the man at the Downtowner, he was a different kind. He was surprising. His eyes were deep-set and the skin cracked in the pockets. His arms wrapped all the way around me and I finally felt small to someone.

He had been around. He knew things. I wanted to know those things. He wrapped his arm underneath me and I tried to like it. My neck was aching, and still nothing was working. He didn't stir as I got up. I went back to my room to lie down and put my head down on my mattress and I inhaled.

"WAKE UP, *DEVOCHKA.*" HE WAS RUBBING ME,

my stomach, kissing me lightly.

"What time is it?" I said.

"Late. I want to take you somewhere."

I had trouble opening my eyes. He kept rubbing. "Where?"

"Wake up, *devochka.*" I could feel him kissing my face and smelled his sour breath. I inhaled deeply while he whispered to me.

I opened my eyes and he was still leaning over me, rubbing me.

"Give me a minute," I said. He walked away and left me alone in my room. I tried to pull it together. I looked at the clock. 4 a.m. I didn't know where we were going so I didn't know how to properly prepare.

"Where are you taking me?" I said. He yelled that it was a surprise. He didn't sound sinister when he said it so I put on a skirt.

When I got into his car I looked around for a sign: a pair of cubic zirconium, clothes, a lost mirror, a pair of women's shoes, a cigarette with a lipstick ring around it snuffed out in the cigarette tray. I made a mental note, listing the possible objects in order of importance. If I were to find... a lost mirror, what would it mean as compared to a pair of earrings? Which loss was more careless? I decided that the shoes would be the worst. They would mean she was coming back.

He pulled out of the street and headed up Fairfax, away from the Twin Palms. He didn't say anything while we drove. I noticed his car smelled new and was spotless, as he turned right on Sunset, toward Little Armenia. He kept everything clean. I wanted to open the glove compartment and so I asked him if there was anything inside. I thought about what I would find, the usual things. Thug things. He told me to open it and I saw that it was vacuumed clean. I decided to stop searching for things then. There was no life in this car.

"Where are we going?"

"Anka, you don't trust. Stop asking."

I stared at who was still walking down the street. There was a man with a backpack walking by the All American Burger; he looked lost, tired, and young. The yellow light from Roscoe's was spilling down Vine and onto Sunset. I wanted to go there but I didn't think Lev would want to so I didn't even ask, and as we passed it, I saw that it was closed anyway. The light flickering, still yellow and bright.

Two women further up the street were sitting on the bench in front of the gas station near Bronson. They were arguing and I couldn't tell if their hair was real. Lev kept driving.

"Anka, where is your family?"

"Texas."

Lev turned to me and smiled. "I've never been to Texas."

"It's not worth going."

He went back to concentrating on driving. "Are there any Polish people there?"

"A Polish ghetto."

"Your family doesn't mix with them?"

"They want to be American so they only mix with Americans."

"And you want to be something else entirely." He looked at me as he said it.

"I don't want to be anything at all." I said it but I didn't mean it. My passing wasn't working and everything was jumbled in my head.

Lev thought about this and I stared at him while he did. I wondered if he could tell I was lying.

"And in Poland? Where are you from?"

I thought about this. City or village. I could say either. I was from both. Well, I had spent time in both. Born in the village, a house with an outhouse, soot-colored walls, and spent the rest of my time in the apartment in the *bloki*.

"Łódź."

"City of Industry," he said.

It used to be. People still walked around with missing limbs, mangled hands, lost in the textile factories. I knew six people with a left arm only. They were old now. The young people didn't work because there were no jobs now, factories long closed. The industry had left the city behind.

"I wouldn't mix with Polish either," he said.

Then, he looked at me and smiled. I snapped out of it and stared at him. He had a gold tooth, back lower right. I hadn't noticed it before because he never really smiled.

"But you are different, Anka."

I smiled at him. I felt like I had won something. I was better. Different. He didn't say better but I thought *better*.

"Where are we going?" I said.

"To my friend's."

He pulled into a strip mall with a beauty supply, a Little Cesar's, a convenience store, and a dry cleaner. There were also a couple of buildings that looked empty and that's where he took me.

He knocked on the door and the shade moved a little. The door opened and we went in. I was glad I was wearing a skirt. The men looked at me like they appreciated it. They were all wearing black leather dusters. Silk shirts. They were sitting around Formica-topped tables and slurping deep red borscht. Women scurried about making sure their plates were full. The florescent overhead made everyone look gray. I stared up at the ceiling not wanting to make eye contact. It was broken up into sheets of stained tile. Lev walked forward and I followed as he sat down at a table in the corner. He said something to the waitress in Russian and she moved away quickly. I sat down and looked around the room. It was all men. Except for me and the women working there. No one looked at us. It made me feel good. It made me feel like I was passing. I mouthed the words of what I saw people eating. Lev studied me while I did. I looked at him and felt self-conscious.

"What?" I said.

"I'm just watching, that's all."

"You have an American accent when you speak Polish, you know?" he continued.

"I didn't."

"It's like a young child's Polish."

"I learned it as a child," I said.

"It's rudimentary."

I looked away. Felt my throat swelling.

"I ordered for us," he said, putting a napkin on his lap.

"You don't know what I wanted." I rubbed my eyes, they were burning and tired.

"They only make one thing good here."

Two soups were set in front of us. There were pieces of meat floating in the borscht. A couple of beans. A slice of cabbage. I saw a bone. I didn't know what this was but I didn't want it. Lev was already eating when I looked up at him. I started eating because I didn't want to offend him. And I hated myself for caring after what he said to me. I ate around the meat and bone. It started out good.

"Do you ever go back to Poland?"

Lev was staring into his soup bowl while he asked. Moving the bones around. Eating the meat.

"Sometimes, I did when I was younger." I was regaining composure. Trying to prove myself to him.

"It's different now."

"Probably not. Things don't change quickly there, thanks to the Communists." I said it slowly but it didn't have the weight I wanted it to.

"Communism helped people like me," he said.

"Why?"

"Not everyone. But me, yes." Lev ripped a piece of bread and put it in the soup and shrugged his shoulders.

"I wouldn't be able to survive there," I said and waited for him to disagree.

"Probably not."

"Maybe I'll try."

"No one should want to leave America. Only the stupid say so."

He quickly changed the subject when he saw me open my mouth and my face turned red.

"And your parents?"

"What about them?"

"They are still here?"

"Of course."

"They don't care that you're so far away?"

"I don't know. I never asked them." I dipped my bread in the soup.

"They stay in their Polish Ghetto in Texas."

"They were never a part of that," I spat out.

I wanted to leave and not have to smell the soup anymore. There were a few beans left, the fatty piece of meat, and the bone. There was gristle on the bone and it was turning my stomach. It must have been 5 a.m. already. The waitresses wandered from table to table and looked sallow and gray-faced. Smokers for sure. Their teeth were gray and thin when they smiled. The florescent lights gave their hair an unnatural tinge. I didn't want to be these women. They spoke hurriedly to the men eating. They were hunched over and old looking but were not old at all. They weren't much older than me.

They just looked like factory girls. The ones who worked the third shift, coming home in the morning, back to the village from the one train that stopped there to let them off on the broken wooden platform, near the edge of the woods. Where they'd walk home to their children and be tired. Drink tea, smoke cigarettes. Crawl into bed and wonder what time their husbands came home the night before. Our waitress brought our check and I stared at her hands. Her nails were thick, cracking at the tips. She opened her mouth to talk and I could see her silver fillings. Lev paid, got up, and touched her back. He held his hand there and I counted the seconds until he took it off. He could feel her bra strap through her cotton shirt and I could tell that it gave her a small thrill. Her first of the night, I thought. He was the most handsome man in this place and she eyed him coyly. As if I wasn't standing beside him.

This wasn't where I wanted to be. This wasn't the Twin Palms. I didn't care about passing anymore. I didn't care about the factory girls. I didn't want to be one of them.

When we got out to the parking lot the cars all had a thin sheet of ash on them. Lev didn't notice. We drove back in silence. I didn't know if he wanted to sleep over and I wasn't sure if I wanted him to. I didn't want his sweat to soil my bare mattress.

"Where do you live?"

"Over the hill," he said.

"Can I see?"

The night was going away and the sky was turning a bright blue. At the horizon it was the bluest, brightest. I wanted to say azure. It was the first time I'd seen it this blue in a long time. It got darker and darker behind me. There was one star and one moon and the palm trees looked black against the sky.

They were long and slender and swayed in step. It looked like a postcard and I wanted to be in it.

He said no. He dropped me off in front of my apartment and said he'd see me later. He kissed me as I fumbled with the door handle. I could taste the soup. I could taste the meat and gristle. The sprinklers were on and I tried not to get my bare legs wet as I got out. He drove away and turned down the street toward the Twin Palms and I knew that's what he was leaving me for.

I RAN AROUND THE TRACK UNTIL I THREW UP.

I think I was there for an hour. Running in circles, making myself dizzy. I stood on the edge of the gravel and stripes and threw everything up. Borscht, hot dogs, carrot cake, bile. I did it until I was heaving and breathing out acrid breaths and there was nothing left inside of me. Teenage girls pointed at me.

They said, "Look at her. She's throwing up."

I told them to shut up and wiped my mouth on my sleeve and kicked gravel over the puke. It didn't cover it at all and I didn't care.

Small hunched women were wrestling with wire carts and going to the little stores that still sold fruit and vegetables in crates on tables, and not in big behemoth refrigerated wall units. Flies filled the air in these shops but their fruit was sweetest. I shopped there all the time. More people seemed to walk on Fairfax than anywhere else, visiting the *apteka*, purchasing orthopedic shoes in discreet black bags, stopping in the grocery and buying cans of food labeled in different languages. Sometimes they walked in packs, sometimes alone, always in layers of clothing – always neat and scrubbed clean. Their appearance was carefully fretted over, even if they walked, nearly bent over in an *L*.

I HAD TO GET READY FOR BINGO. IT STARTED

at 7 p.m. but they were already circling at 4:30, waiting in the foyer of Holy Virgin and fingering their bingo chips, their blotters. I took a shower and did my hair. The roots were coming in again. I'd have to get another box of color. I was thinking darker. Raven-like this time. I wanted to add to my mystery. I wanted my eyes to glow and my skin to look luminescent. Like in the Cover Girl commercials I was seeing. The new thing was Vamp. I think Lev would like it. It would look Russian, maybe Siberian, and it would look good against fur. I had a vision of myself and I liked it.

I stopped at the pharmacy before I went to the Holy Virgin. I picked out a color called "Black Stilettos." It sounded thrilling and dangerous. I wanted to dye my hair immediately but I had obligations. Mary had all her bingo boards laid out in front of her when I got there. She was wearing a red sweatshirt with bows all over it. Gold lamé, silver, she liked looking festive for her nights out. She waved me over.

"Come here, you," she said.

I walked over and sat down.

"What's with the new cards this week?"

I wasn't in charge of the cards but she always brought her problems to me.

"I don't know anything about them."

"They're martini glasses. We're supposed to get bingo in martini shapes instead of diamonds. We were just getting used to the diamonds and now this."

I had no idea what she was talking about. I was staring at the picture of her husband in a small, dirty frame. She only had pictures of him from when he was young. I've never seen him old, her age, and I couldn't imagine him being dead. He lived in small picture frames with sepia tones and striking jaw-lines and a nose like a boxer and wavy 1950s slicked-back hair. He was handsome and he looked like a man. A man I wanted to know. A man I had never seen before. Even Lev wasn't a man like he was. He was different. Mary was lucky. She caught me staring and took the picture and stuffed it in between her breasts. Her sweatshirt hugged him, enveloped him. "He's mine."

She took him out from between her breasts and kissed him. Over and over again. She had two birds on the table. Lovebirds. She had them kissing. She moved one behind the other.

"He's doing her up the back skull."

I stopped for a minute. "What?" I said.

I thought I didn't hear her right.

"He's doing her up the back skull." She giggled when she said it. "Do you and your honey do that? Up the back skull?"

"I don't have a honey, Mary," I said.

"That's too bad. My honey did." She went back to kissing his picture.

"I have to go call the numbers, Mary." The women were already pushing their cards around and glaring at me. Waiting for me to get on with it.

"Let me win this week," Mary said as I walked away. She moved the birds back to the kissing position as I climbed up the stairs toward the big bingo board and took a seat.

"Hello, are we ready to get started?" I called out, smiling. I only got grumbles back.

"We're starting with the regular game today. And we've got a new one… Martini glass. That's coming up later." More grumbles. I had to up the ante.

"Two Twizzlers with your money. Maybe even an éclair." I heard a hoot.

"This is the Early Bird special, ladies. Let's get ready. Regular bingo and 4 corners wins. Then full card for sixty dollars."

I turned on the ball machine and watched the balls begin roiling through the air.

"O 69." I heard more hoots. A few moans. Table bells ringing. This was their game. They loved when I called 69. I cringed. The sea of white-colored heads bobbed over their boards. One woman screamed out a fat man's name after I said 69. He was at the table with the hot dogs and éclairs. I saw him blushing. He opened a bag of Doritos and ate. I tried to move on, regroup, and get their minds off of 69's.

"I 16."

There was a ruckus in the corner. I saw Mary waving her cane at the Mexican lady who took up the corner table. She was surrounded by small plastic toys – penguins, rabbits, lions. I leaned into the microphone while holding a bingo ball.

"What's going on there, ladies?"

Mary looked up at me. So did the Mexican lady. They yelled something but I couldn't hear over the whir of the bingo balls.

"Let's keep going with the game. Sixty dollars on this board. Lucky 13 doubles your money today. Sit down, Mary."

She did, but I could tell she wasn't happy about it. She waved her cane at the woman. I saw her mouth "twat." The priest came up to Mary and tried to calm her down.

"B 5." I saw Mary making flirty eyes with Father Ford and I knew it was going to be okay. She batted her eyelashes at him.

Men took her mind off things.

Mary didn't win. When I came up to her afterward she looked pissed.

"I was going to shove my cane up her twat."

"What'd she do?"

"She's loud and I don't like her."

"Sit somewhere else next time."

"I could stick it up there. She has a big one." She leaned in when she told me that. Like she was telling me a secret.

"I'm sorry."

"It's the birds. Next week I'm just bringing the picture."

"I didn't see Carla."

"Who the fuck knows where she is." She looked up at me and smiled. "Did I tell you what I saw yesterday?"

"No, Mary. What'd you see?"

"A man, sitting in his car. Jerking off."

I looked at her and shook my head. "In front of your house?"

"In front of my house. I went to the kitchen. Came back he was still at it…"

She looked past me. At the painted concrete wall of the multi-purpose room. "Looked like a big one too. He was going in and out like this." She made the motion with her hand. She leaned in close. "It turned me on. It really did."

I tried not to seem disturbed.

"It got me hot and bothered. It looked big."

"Wow," was all I could come up with and that made her laugh.

"I'm going to hell. I know it."

I started walking away and all I could hear was her laughter. I tried to clean up. Get my money. I wanted to get out of there and put Black Stilettos in my hair, get away from Mary's laughter. I put the bingo boards away, tried to get the chairs in order, get the women out and onto their buses. The drivers looked tired; the women were wearing them down too. I went back in to finish cleaning and saw Mary still sitting there.

"Mary, you missed the buses."

She looked up, looked upset, maybe confused. "I didn't know they were here." She started getting up, using her cane. She had already put away her cards, her chips, and her birds. The picture was still on the table. I ran to see if I could catch the buses but they were all gone. Everyone was. It was just me and Mary. She was sweating when I got back and she looked nervous.

"How am I going to get home?"

The big electronic bingo board had already been turned off and looked worn out and outdated. They were starting to turn off the lights and I knew that I couldn't leave her.

"I can take you home, Mary."

Neither of us wanted it but we both moved toward my car anyway.

I had to move the seat back for Mary. Her cane, bag, and everything else wouldn't fit.

"I think you should change back the games to the way they used to be. I don't like the new ones."

"I just call the numbers, Mary. I don't choose the games."

"You're all in it together against us."

I started the car and she looked away from me. Out the window.

"Where do you live?"

"Just drive this way. I'll show you the rest."

I told her I was sorry she didn't win.

"I have to get out of the house. Otherwise, I just walk from room to room missing him."

She paused for a moment.

"But I keep a clean house, honey." She pointed her long frosted fingernail at me while she said it.

I didn't want to look at her. I couldn't.

"Why don't you have someone? You're not ugly. Anyone can get someone."

I tried to pull apart what she said. There was no way to answer. So, I just said, I don't know.

I also said, "I'm trying."

"Women shouldn't have to try. Even at the end, when he

couldn't get more than soft. He felt so terrible. He would cry. But he was mine and I told him it was okay."

It took me a moment to understand what she was saying.

"Turn left at that light."

"I'm sure he loved you very much."

"I'll show you my wedding photos. You're pretty, but I was beautiful."

I shook my head. I couldn't even compete with an 82-year-old.

"I want it all back again. I want someone again. Not someone old and soft. I want someone young and hard."

She told me to turn right. I was struggling to keep up.

"You need someone strong like a bull. Someone to fuck you up the back skull. We all do."

She sighed. I didn't want to imagine anyone doing that to her. But for a second I imagined Lev doing that to me. With her sitting next to me as I thought about it, I started feeling sick. And then I thought about the man in room 214. It was nice, for a moment, to go there.

"You've already had it." It was the first time I could talk, when I thought she'd actually listen.

"I have."

"You don't have to look for it anymore. Some people don't even get it once."

"I had it."

"Things like that don't exist anymore," I said, testing her.

"They never did," she said. She thought about it for a moment. "There are things… you can't possibly know."

She said it fast, not like it was profound or anything. Just like that. It wasn't to her. It wasn't to me either, I guess.

"Did I tell you what I saw yesterday?" she said.

She asked me to pull up to a house. It was blue stucco and the plants outside were wilting and overgrown. I didn't know how she was going to get up the stairs, if she was going to ask me to help her and I knew I didn't want to.

She turned around to face me.

"What?" I said.

"A man, sitting right here –"

"Oh yeah, you did," I said.

She smiled at me. Like I knew just what she was talking about. "You'll always want it, honey. And it's worse when you've had it and it's gone."

She pushed her cane out.

"Maybe I can pay you to clean my gutters. And my plants. Look at my plants. I'm just one woman. He did it all for me."

The lights in her house were already on. I didn't want to clean her gutters. I didn't want to go inside. I wasn't sure I ever wanted to see her again.

"I want to show you how pretty I was. Come on."

I waited a moment. She wasn't waiting for me. She was already turning the key to her door. She turned and stood in the doorway and I knew I had to go in. I turned off the car.

THERE WERE PICTURES OF HORSES ALL OVER

Mary's walls. Mustangs running in packs through the American West, single horses with saddles looking regal and staring off into space, wall-to-wall brown carpeting, and dust. She also had religious statues everywhere and I was surprised she let me in. She didn't know me. This was her place and not mine. She had a full-sized Virgin Mary with a blue gown like we had when I was young. Her Mary had a chipped face and a broken hand and cobwebs around the base of her.

"Wait here," she said.

She wandered away from me and I looked around some more. The windows were covered in yellowing lace curtains. Like my grandmother in Poland. Like all the grandmothers in Poland.

She came back with an armload of photos and ordered me to sit down. She spread them out before me and she was right. She was beautiful. I looked at her now and I looked at her then, her dress cascading down, looped around the floor and ruffled at the bottom. She was standing on stairs next to him, her husband, and she looked ten feet tall, a redheaded statue with sharp brows and red lips. She was a sexpot. She was all I needed to be.

"Mary, you were a redhead," I said.

"Always. I was hot. Fiery."

She touched her husband's face. "It wasn't every Tom, Dick,

Harry, and Joe." She turned her face toward me. "It was only him. He popped my cherry. One man."

She stuck her index finger in my face and then pointed at the picture. "One man."

She wasn't looking at herself. She was looking at him. He was smiling and holding her and in the photo she had a look on her face like she had won. She had tears in her eyes and I knew she wanted to be alone with him and I got up to leave.

"Give me your number, for the gutters," she said as I stood up.

I did, even though I didn't want to clean her gutters, and left her alone. I walked to my car and I knew she was crying in there. I felt her loneliness and wanted it. I wanted hers. I didn't want mine anymore.

IT WAS GOING TO BE RED. NOT BLACK. I

wanted to get her kind of red. That copper, that sheen. That curl. I threw the box of Black Stilettos out the window and started over. The pharmacy was closed when I drove by it so I kept driving. I passed the Downtowner. The desk clerk was standing there. He was staring through the window, out onto the street, and he didn't recognize me. I was glad. He looked prim, older in his uniform than he really was. I looked at the slip of the pool, no one was in it. Was room 214 still occupied? I slowed down and turned onto a street nearby, sitting in my car for a while. Room 214 was better, it was different, new. Untethered. I got out of my car and walked toward the gate, opened it, and stood next to the pool. The desk clerk looked up, saw me, shook his head, and looked back at the blue glow of his television. The light wasn't on in 214. I considered asking the desk clerk and thought better of it. He didn't have any answers. I sat down in a broken-down plastic chair and waited. I wanted it to be like the other night. It wasn't going to be, though. I knew it.

"He left early."

I didn't have to turn around to know the desk clerk had come outside.

"He's a firefighter," he said quietly.

Was he missing Room 214 too? I heard the scrape of a chair and closed my eyes. We waited and he never came. He was after the fires too. I knew he did something important, I could tell.

WHEN THE BANGING ON MY DOOR BEGAN LATE

in the night I didn't open it right away. But I saw lights turning on and knew it was loud and knew he wasn't going to leave. I went and opened the door. He pushed in, didn't let me see his face and went into the bathroom, shutting the door behind him. I went back to my room and closed the door. I heard him running water, searching through cabinets. I didn't care. I closed my eyes.

"Anya, I need you." There was an urgency in his voice that I hadn't heard before. My room was dark and the light behind him in the doorway made him look big. I got up and started moving toward him and he went back into the bathroom.

"I need something for my face."

I didn't want to ask him. His cheek was swollen and scratched. He looked annoyed, his hair was disheveled and he kept opening cabinets.

"Sit down." He did what I said and sat on the toilet. He jiggled his foot as he waited. I pulled what I needed together. Cotton balls, alcohol… I eyed his face. Vaseline. I leaned in to him as he sat on the toilet and soaked the cotton ball. I dabbed his face and he closed his eyes. I could tell it stung and I was glad. He hissed at me.

"What happened?" I finally asked.

"My wife scratched me."

My face felt fuzzy. I squeezed the cotton ball against his face and the alcohol escaped and ran down his cheek. He grabbed it away from me, wiped his face. "What are you doing?"

I backed away from him and was scared of him for the first time. He dabbed his cheek. He wouldn't look at me.

"We got into fight. She gets upset."

The words kept coming. I wasn't listening. I stood in the doorway and watched him. The fuzziness wasn't going away. He opened the Vaseline and squeezed too much out. He smeared it on his face.

"You're not doing it right."

"Do it for me then."

"No." I walked away. Closed my bedroom door again. I put my head down on my pillow and waited to stop hearing his sounds.

"Anya." He came in and crawled into bed beside me. "You still have no sheets."

I rolled over and tried to get away from him.

"I have to stay here a couple of days."

"No."

He pulled me close. Wrapped his arm around me and kissed my neck.

"No," I said.

He wasn't listening.

THE NEXT DAY, I GOT UP AND LEFT HIM SLEEP-

ing on my mattress. I stood on the balcony smoking and wondered what I had done. My neighbor came up to me. I didn't want to talk to him but I hadn't thanked him for the mackerel yet.

"Did you like?" His mustache was newly trimmed. Too nipped in at the sides. He smiled at me and really wanted me to like it.

"It was delicious."

"I made for you. My mother said you would like."

I smiled at him and sucked in my cigarette. "It was delicious."

"Did you watch out for the bones? I was afraid you choked."

I thought about it. The bronzed skin of the mackerel. The foggy eyes, the slit stomach, the brown meat. I hadn't eaten it but I had studied it. The scales looked gilded and I touched them, smoke smell on my fingertips. I had stuck my fingers inside the stomach, touched the flesh and slid my fingers over the ribs, breaking up the meat.

"I didn't choke."

He stood there smiling at me. I didn't know what else to say so I told him it was delicious, again. He walked over to his mother's balcony and pulled himself over the ledge. He opened the curtains and I saw her portraits. Old faces, black-and-white 8 x 10 photos lining the walls – hardened faces, mothers and fathers, dark suits, staring out into the living room. She had them all edging the ceiling. On all the walls, looking down into the living room with disdain. She brought the village to Los Angeles. I wanted to steal her photos. I wanted to line my walls with them. I thought about the village. My family in the village. My cousin with permed maroon hair. I helped her perm it once when we visited them. I was thirteen and stained my hands because I didn't know better yet. The box had a smiling woman with curly hair and the chemicals smelled horrible. I wound her hair tightly around the curlers. They were rubbery and light green and I wondered how old the box was.

My cousin had a garden in her front yard. There were Gerbera daisies and lines of flowers in her small plot. Her sister was named Jagoda and had Down's Syndrome and she lived there too. Jagoda wore skirts and smiled and sunned herself in the garden. My cousin was married to a man who liked to drink and sometimes he crawled into the wrong bed at night. Jagoda didn't say anything but my cousin knew and she wasn't going to leave him. They didn't do that there. They had our family members in pictures lining the walls and watching them. They had chickens in their backyards and mushrooms drying in their cellar. I liked to walk down there and smell the air. Thick with forest mushrooms and dirt. It was cold down there and I felt alone and I liked it. Jagoda never went downstairs. She didn't like the dark.

When I left they all stood in the garden and waved at me. Jagoda stepped on some flowers and my cousin scolded her. Her husband just watched me go and waved heartily. Jagoda looked down at her feet, at the flowers pressed into the ground and bit her lip. She looked up and started waving again. Forgetting what she had done. My cousin turned around and walked back into the house. Did anyone else know what I knew?

I passed the graveyard in the middle of the village and saw old women washing the headstones. It was Saturday. The graveyards were filled. Women in *chustki* lined the dirt walkways between the headstones. Kneeling, praying, scrubbing, changing flowers, holding rosaries, and rocking back and forth. Rubbing on the headstones of their dead husbands. They rubbed their hands raw cleaning the headstones.

Before I left we had gone to the church where my parents had been married. It was quiet, empty. When I closed the door behind me I closed out the sound of the roosters in the front yard across the street, and my cousins chattering in the garden. I walked inside and tried to think about how it was back then. There was an altar and it was covered in food. Glistening bread sculptures. Round, brown, and shining. *Babki* in the form of roosters, cows, and sheep. All on the altar as an offering, the farmers begging for a good crop. There were dried corn stalks leaning against the altar, baskets of apples, potatoes. I stared at it all. They were offering up their food to make more food. I thought about Easter in the Polish church in America. People bringing in baskets with colored eggs, white sausage, salt, pepper, chocolates. Some had lottery tickets peeking out in between sausages and eggs. The priest would come around throwing his holy water at us. We'd cross ourselves. The other Polish people would cross themselves and stare down at their lotto tickets. In this church in Poland there were no lottery tickets stuck around the altar. Just the food and the Black Madonna staring down, cut on her face, holding her son. Gold crown. I stared at the cut in her face. I heard the door open again and knew it was time to go. We walked by the cemetery again. My family was buried there and there were spaces for me and my parents too.

They weren't coming back to be buried here but I wasn't sure yet. The women had stayed hunched over the headstones, cleaning and shining while I walked by.

My neighbor closed her curtains and I couldn't see the

pictures anymore. It was Saturday. I knew the women were washing and rubbing headstones today, in Poland.

I walked into my apartment and went back into my bedroom. It was early evening and Lev was still in and out of sleep. I crawled next to him. He tucked me into his arm and pulled me close. It felt nice. I liked his warmth as he breathed into my neck and it felt familiar. I wanted to forget about his wife. He was here, not with her, and that meant something to me.

Later, his phone started to ring. He didn't answer it at first. But it kept ringing and ringing. He finally stirred and got it. He yelled in Russian and grunted, got up and walked out of the room. I knew who it was and when he closed the door to my bedroom and walked away from me I knew I wasn't winning anything. He came back in and started putting on his pants. He said some things in Russian. I didn't want to say anything, yet. He paced around the room and then sat down. I didn't want him to say it.

"Bitch."

I was happy. It wasn't what I thought he was going to say.

"I have to go."

My face fell. He saw. I didn't want him to, but he did.

"I have to go. She took my car."

He put his dress shirt on. It was crinkled. I knew where he was going and I was going to go too. I was just going to wait for a bit.

He left me and I pretended like I was going to stay in bed. I heard the front door close and I got up. I went to the bathroom to fix myself up. The box color said Spicy Ginger. I put on the plastic gloves and mixed the mixture. It stunk but I was used to it. I painted it on, dripped on the bathmat and moaned. Thirty-five minutes of waiting. I put on a shower cap and caught myself in the mirror. I looked ridiculous but this was it. I knew this was what I finally needed. I would look ravishing, fresh, and new. I could start over again and try harder this time. I would ask more of people.

I showered, washed the dye out of my hair, watched it trail down the shower curtain, shaved my legs and armpits. I cut my ankle while I was shaving. I watched the blood slide down my foot. It hurt like hell. Lev had a wife.

I got out of the shower and the blood was still coming out of my ankle. I didn't try and stop it. It got on the bathmat too. I trailed it through the apartment, onto the Berber carpet. I opened a bottle of wine and went from room to room drinking from the glass. Bleeding on the rug. I tracked it everywhere. I hadn't sufficiently washed all the dye out of my hair and it was dripping everywhere too. I didn't care. I already knew I wouldn't get my deposit back. I had done too much here.

When I walked out of my apartment I had tight pants, push-up bra in place, and my hair red and fiery. The crocheted curtains across the street moved and the apartment lights glowed in the darkness. I walked down the street and over to the Twin Palms. I didn't know what I would do but I saw myself walking up the stairs and knew I was doing it. I was walking up the stairs and stared at myself in the mirrored wall. The color was good. The light from the streetlamps behind me made it glow like a halo. I heard talking. I walked slowly, the stairs creaked, and I walked slower. I started breathing again and when I got to the top step of the stairs I turned left and saw the wall of frosted glass. There was a light show reflecting on it. I wasn't sure what it was supposed to be, a neon pitter-patter of raindrops? I didn't know what kind of effect they were going for. There were cut-outs in the frost of the glass and I leaned forward, trying to look through. A man in a dress shirt walked up the stairs smoking a cigarette. He was staring down at the carpet and didn't see me peering through the glass until he was almost on top of me. I turned around and smiled at him. He inhaled his cigarette and looked me up and down. I spoke quickly.

"I've never been up here. Is it a restaurant?"

"It's for special events only," he said.

"Oh." I looked at him. Stood against the frost. "I always pass by. I live in the neighborhood. It looked interesting."

"I'll let you in for 100 dollars."

I turned and looked through the glass, as much as I could see. Nothing was happening in there. "For what?"

"Private party – 100 is for all the free vodka you can have."

"I don't see anyone in there."

"You come back later with 100 dollars, I'll let you in. You look like you could have fun here."

I smiled. Maybe I had been wasting my time with Lev. The fact was still that I didn't have 100 dollars to wander in alone. It wasn't the same. "Can I just look inside?"

He nodded. "For 100 dollars."

"It's okay. Thank you."

He wouldn't let me pass. Almost pushed his groin against me as I walked past the railing to get back downstairs.

"Bring money back and I show you around." He winked at me when he said it and I wish Lev had seen him do it. I wondered if he'd strike him or not.

I walked down the carpeted stairs as quickly as I could and ran down the street. Lev wouldn't have struck him. I knew that.

I got into my car and started driving. I saw myself in the rearview mirror and moved up, checked out my torso, pushed my boobs down. I drove toward the smoke, toward the fires.

I drove on the 5 along the L.A. River. It was empty except for a trickle. We were having a drought, again. There were trees in the middle of the river. Graffiti on the sides. Corrugated roofs and low warehouses on the other side. I never came over here. I didn't like it. Sitting in traffic I watched the water move slowly, watched people with carts walk along the side of it, along the concrete, a dull, fake yellow under the freeway lights and orange sky. The smoke was filling the sky in front of me. I thought I should have a mask on for where I was going but it was too late to get off the highway. I didn't know my way around Glendale or Burbank and was afraid I'd get lost.

Where did Lev live?

This was over the hill. This was the valley, where he pointed to when I asked him to take me home. Did he and his wife live in a beige stucco house? Fenced in and valley sensible?

It didn't matter. I was getting closer to the fires. I saw them on the sides of the freeway. I saw fire trucks in the distance. I wasn't sure how close they were going to let me go but I was going to push it. I wanted to get close to the fires too.

I saw fire jump over the road and go to the other side and crawl up a tree. The hills were smoldering. Everything was charred and black. Trees were black and gnarled and had charred nubs for limbs. They were detouring us, the only cars left on the freeway. I moved along with the cars and didn't know where I was. The smoke was thick and I was on a road that had flares on it and there were policemen with smoke masks waving us on and pushing into the hills. Firefighters too. They rushed past, toward the fires, and I craned my neck to see past the masks. I put my windshield wipers on. The ash was coming down like rain and I couldn't see. I opened the windows and started to cough. I needed a mask. I rolled the windows back up. They were stopping the cars in front of me, asking where they were going. I had no answer when it was my turn and coughed out the window at the policeman. I was directed to make a three-point turn and head back to the 5 and back to Los Angeles. There was no place for me here. I wasn't trying to save my home or go to the shelter. The policeman frowned. He didn't know what I was up to, but he didn't like it, made me drive back down the interstate. I couldn't get my bearings straight.

I took the 170 to the 101 and headed back to Hollywood. Past the car dealerships and the mosque, the deaf children's school. Nothing made sense anymore. The giant neon cross on the hill was leaning down toward me. I opened the window and breathed in the air. It was blowing in my face and it felt fresh and I felt like I was flying. I accelerated and when I saw red taillights in front of me I quickly pulled off the freeway onto an exit, careful not to lose my stride.

THE HOLLYWOOD DOWNTOWNER WASN'T ON

my way home but I went anyway and the ash was thicker in the pool now. The desk clerk had stopped trying to clean it. It was coming down harder now, harder than the last time I was here, but I didn't care. I didn't want to go home. None of the lights were on in the rooms, I tried to glaze my eyes over 214. The pool was bright blue, lights shining up and breaking through the film of ash. I took my shoes off and sat at the edge of the pool and stuck my legs in. It felt cool. I got up and took my clothes off but kept my bra and panties and climbed on the diving board and started to bounce. Hanging down over the water I wanted a space to open up, to not have the ash. The board was old and creaked with each bounce. The light clicked on in 214 and I jumped into the water and went under, broke through the ash and swam around under the water until my lungs hurt. I stared up at the surface and saw ash closing up the hole I had made and saw the desk clerk running around on the side. I stayed down a few more seconds to make him sweat, to have a dramatic rise to the surface. I let air bubbles rise up first, and then I followed.

"Are you okay? Are you hurt?"

I opened my eyes and smiled at him. He didn't recognize me at first and then he did.

"What are you doing here?"

"I'm swimming."

"You can't just *do* that."

"No one's here."

"You don't know that," he said.

The door opened to room 214 and we both inhaled sharply. He was coming down with a towel and this time I would ask more probing questions.

I swam around the middle and waited. He sat down in one of the poolside chairs near the desk clerk, who said something to him I couldn't hear. I went under again. I swam toward the bottom, as far as I could go and touched the rough bottom and stayed there until I couldn't anymore. Then shot myself up, back to the surface.

The desk clerk was folding my clothes and putting them on the table. It seemed too intimate to me. Room 214 was watching me now. I considered putting on a show for him, some elaborate swim thing. Instead, I crawled closer to them, twisting my legs to the side as I moved, trying to look stretched and lean.

"No. Business has been slow. The fires," the desk clerk said. I hadn't heard Room 214 ask a question. He looked tired again.

"I wish they were closer," I said.

They both looked at me strangely.

I went back to tread water in the middle, away from them.

"They're killing business."

"They're leveling everything out," I said.

I waited for Room 214 to say something. He looked at me like he understood, or maybe I was just making that up.

I swam closer to him. It was nice to be here, somewhere else in the city that had no ownership on me. Room 214 was just someone else, but I was in control here. Doing what I wanted, pulling the pool water and ash into my mouth and then spitting it back out again.

"Maybe it is," Room 214 said.

The phone rang and the desk clerk hesitated, then ran.

"Are you coming in?" I asked.

Room 214 looked at me and shook his head. "I'm too tired to kick."

"You can stand still in here, let the ash circle around you."

"I've been getting that enough." He narrowed his eyes at me. "You like fire that much?"

"No. I mean, no."

We squared off, eye to eye, until he took off his shirt and jumped in, not even afraid of the cold. I knew what he was asking.

We swam around each other for a while, he kicked fine. I tried to stay in the deep end and he paced back and forth, creating small dips and waves.

"Someone should clean the pool," he said.

"The desk clerk doesn't like to do it."

"His name is Jason."

"What's your name?" I said.

"Greg."

Greg, Greg, Greg. How boring. He didn't seem playful or prone to deceit. He probably had a wife but I didn't see a ring. He didn't ask my name. It didn't seem important to him.

"Are you fighting the Moorpark and the Tierra Rejada?"

"Excuse me?"

"Which fire are you fighting? You're here for the fires, right?"

"I don't know what it's called. The bigger one."

"Tierra Rejada," I said breathlessly.

"What's your problem?" he asked.

I wasn't sure how to answer.

"I don't know, what's yours?" I said.

"This place. This place doesn't make sense to me."

"It's all right. Takes some getting used to." I let pool water into my mouth and pushed it out again, for effect. "There are places you should see."

"Why would you live somewhere where there's fires, floods, and mudslides all the time? Earthquakes."

He raised his hands up when he said earthquakes. Like it was so stupid he couldn't comprehend it.

"Those are the seasons here," I said. Holding out my hand and letting the ash crinkle into it.

I was getting defensive now.

"Are you really from Oklahoma?" I asked.

"Yeah."

"What's it like?" I asked.

"It's flat."

"I used to think Los Angeles was flat. I believed it was flat," I said. I stared at the hills and felt foolish.

"I think everyone does at first," he said. "Then you get trapped here and you know better."

I stared up at the hills and thought about being trapped and if the mountain ranges around us made me feel caved in. With the ash falling faster, I thought about the mountains pushing us down and the fires doing the rest.

"I guess they're trying to shake us loose, get us out of here."

"Who's they?" he asked.

"I don't know," I said quietly.

"Well, think about it. No one wants any of you here."

I thought about it.

"And all that kindling up there? Poof. You bastards don't even make it easy on yourselves. *Just clear it.*"

I didn't know him well enough for him to yell at me like that. But he was making sense. All of us, roaming, maybe Los Angeles didn't want us here either. She was trying to shake us free, scorch us out and start over.

But… he seemed somewhat nihilistic.

He was staring at the persistent ash, but not going underneath it. Maybe that would make him feel better. I told him so, but he just shook his head. I asked him to tell me more about the fires, the worst ones he'd seen. How they started.

He looked at me strangely. "Your hair's different. I didn't recognize you at first."

"Box color."

"Whatever it is, it's nice. Suits you."

I nodded like I knew it was true. I noticed the change of subject on his part and knew he wasn't going to tell me more. I would have to find out for myself.

"They're moving me tomorrow. I have to go tell him." He pointed at Jason, the desk clerk.

"Where?" I said it with too much urgency and rushed out of the water.

"Simi Valley, I think. Closer. There's no point me being here, if it's over there."

"Maybe it'll get closer."

"Doubtful."

"But then it'd make sense for you to be here."

He thought about it for a moment.

Then he mouthed something like *catastrophic*. He held the last bit. The *-phic*, really drawing it out.

He was going closer to the fire and I wanted to go too.

He started getting up to talk to Jason. I put a towel around myself and looked up at room 214. I didn't want him to forget me so I ran up the stairs and grabbed the railing hard as I went. He had left the door ajar.

His room had a thin brown carpet, floral comforter from a shiny kind of synthetic material. It didn't look like it had ever been washed. He had a bag in the corner. It looked jocky, childish. Like a giant gym bag. I went over quickly and peered inside. Underwear. Pants. A pile of white cotton undershirts getting wrinkled. I had an urge to fold them but there was no time. I had to make a list. I found a pad of paper. Downtowner in atomic black lettering across the top. A pen in the drawer, the end chewed to a nub. I didn't care.

I scrawled:

<u>things to do when in la</u>
(I underlined for effect)
go to the beach. zuma beach. trancas market. salty tortilla chips
– greasy ← so what.
top of laurel canyon, left at mulholland, right into the park.
stand there until it gets dark. Longer.
Top of building. A roof somewhere. Just look.
Go to chinatown. late. Full House. orange chicken. Go sit in the
square. Digest. Listen to the mah jong through the door.

I was worried he was coming and I was running out of things.
Jamba juice? Everything was gone.

Snow white cottages
take the curves around the reservoir.
Tommy's. It's near.
Then Galcos. It's far.
Observatory. Crawl down the side to the Greek. There's a path.

I thought I heard voices. I threw the pen, and my wet fingertips rippled the cheap paper as I put the notepad neatly on his
clothes and peeked out the window. He was still talking to Jason
by the glass-squared office. I quietly ran out the door. And away.
I hoped he would follow my directions.

I WOKE UP ON MY BLANK MATTRESS TO THE

phone ringing. My hair was still damp, but the underwear I had swam in were dry. Flakes of ash dotted them, and they were crinkled and uncomfortable.

"Hello?"

"Zosia."

I exhaled. I couldn't do this right now. "Mother."

"Zosia, where have you been? You don't answer."

I didn't want to open my eyes and wake up.

"Answer me."

"Working a lot."

"You could call. I'm lonely."

She tried to hide her accent or maybe I was used to it and couldn't hear it anymore.

"I'm sorry."

"Are you sleeping?"

"Yeah, I was."

She informed me that it was 11 o'clock on a Monday. Work time. I hated lying to her and was bad at it. I backpedaled and told her I was sick, just today but I'd be back to work for the entire week. She asked me how the unemployment service was, how it felt to be helping people. I lied and told her it was the best work I had done in a long time, the sense of pride I felt helping people. I was living the American dream.

"You are getting people off welfare. That is the worst you can be in this country. Taking handouts."

I didn't want to tell her that I had been taking handouts for months. It would only depress her. Her immigrant guilt was too much for me.

"We only took handouts once. And not money. Just clothes. Nothing else."

"I know, Mother, I know."

"Did you go to church?"

I was silent. I thought about telling her about the Holy Virgin, converting bingo nights into 3-hour church service, me on the pulpit, calling numbers, helping the wounded widows of the Holy Virgin forget about their deceased husbands.

"What kind of woman do you hope to be if you don't go to church?" she asked.

"Are you there?"

"I feel dizzy," I said.

"Church. One hour each Sunday is not a lot to ask, Zosia. And yet you can't even do that."

We have been through this before. Every Sunday. It was Monday and she caught me. I hadn't talked to her in weeks after she had told me I was failing as a woman. Unable to bring religion into the home, that was why I couldn't find a husband. That is why I was a failure as a woman. I tried not to think about all of these things as I rolled from one side of my mattress to the other, trying to catch a passing hint of Lev. Trying to get the smell of chlorine off of me. I couldn't understand why I hadn't taken a shower last night. It was unlike me.

"You will never be happy."

I started listening again. I liked listening to what she had to say about the happiness-is-religion equation. It was always ridiculous to me, but she believed it wholeheartedly.

"Who says I'm unhappy?" I asked.

"You don't go to church, how can you be happy? You are just a user. You give nothing back."

"You just said how happy you were about my giving unemployed people a job."

"It's not the same, you're empty without God. No one can do anything themselves. And you choose to go alone. You'll never make it."

"I will."

"It's too hard," she said.

"I know."

"See. You prove it," she said. But that wasn't what I meant.

"I'll go this week."

"Don't do it for me."

"You usually call on Sunday mornings," I said.

"Your grandfather's anniversary is today."

This is why I kept away from her, why I didn't like talking to her. She would never give him peace.

I thought about my grandfather. He was dead, a few years dead. She still celebrated his death every year at the same time. A day in August I could and could not forget. *Celebrate* isn't the right word. Held vigil, something religious and sacred.

She wasn't even there. I was. She had spent his last few days in Poland "collecting herself." When my grandfather had to be restrained I had to tie his arms down. He was incoherent and moaning. There was terrycloth fabric on the inside of the restraints, to "add comfort." He would have pulled out his catheter otherwise; there was evidence of this on the ceiling of his room. Nantucket beadboard covered in blood and urine, caked on thick and in a snake-like shape. I always tried not to look up at it. I was afraid it would drip down on me, even though it'd been dry up there for weeks. Why hadn't anyone cleaned it? He continued to moan in Polish. He wasn't even forming words anymore and I wasn't sure what to do. I undid the restraints and he stopped moaning. He stopped looking at me like I was his tormenter. The silver teeth that had been glinting in the hallway light closed shut in his mouth.

I backed away from the bed and went into the living room, onto the sofa and waited for silence. For the small moans to subside, for the snores to begin, for him to stop mumbling in Polish and begging for my dead grandmother. I fell asleep after there was silence in his room and woke up abruptly when I heard a low growl. I was scared to look but forced myself.

He was sitting on the edge of his bed. Colostomy bag open and shit on the floor and covering his hands. He looked at me and offered it to me like a gift, held out his shit-covered hands and smiled his hollow-mouth smile. He couldn't understand English so I had to yell at him in Polish.

"*Co ty robisz?*" was all I could say, over and over again. I took it all from him and threw it in the sink. She wasn't there to help me and I wouldn't be able to get that smell off my hands for weeks. I kept them in my pockets whenever I could.

THE POLISH CHURCH WAS ON WEST ADAMS

and was nothing like the cathedral in Częstochowa. The church had cheap beams criss-crossing the ceiling, a cramped, hot interior. Only their copy of the Black Madonna stood out. Her black face, gold bejeweled crown, ornate robe, the scar on her face, her wound. I liked to look at it. I liked to think about seeing the real thing in Poland and the pebbles eating into my knees as I crawled around the altar in prayer like everyone else who had made the pilgrimage to this holy place, passing the face of the Black Madonna, chanting and praying for forgiveness. This church had a fading, framed poster of Pope John Paul II beside The Black Madonna and old women bent over their rosaries, praying in Polish, moaning the words of Our Father. It reminded me of the women in the graveyards in Poland, the grave cleaners, the tombstone washers. They had lace *chustki* on their heads, some black, some white. They clutched each bead on their rosary and went through the words.

> *I odpuść nam nasze winy,*
> *jako i my odpuszczamy naszym winowajcom.*
> *I nie wódź nas w pokuszenie,*
> *ale nas zbaw ode złego*

Forgive us our trespasses as we forgive those who trespass against us and lead us not into temptation, but deliver us from evil.

I remember the words in Polish from church as a child; they were numbing. I liked to hear them and not add in my English version. I liked to stumble along in Polish. *Winy* sounded like veen-eh, like *vino*, like wine, but were trespasses. Sins. I prayed for my grandfather's soul. I prayed that he wasn't seeing what I was doing but I wondered if he could. I wanted to stop thinking about it so I started praying harder.

WHEN I LEFT THE CHURCH I HAD A MISSED CALL

on my phone. It was Mary. The gutters. They needed to be cleaned and she didn't know what to do about it. I didn't know either. I wasn't sure if I knew how to get back to her house. I only knew it passed the Downtowner motel and so I took a different route. Down Franklin with palm trees buckling over and high-rise apartments built in the '70s where I heard women who had sex for money lived. They had the nicest views and wall-to-wall Berber carpeting. I liked knowing where the sex workers lived in Los Angeles. I felt like it gave me cache, let me know secrets other people didn't know. I don't even know how I knew this fact, but I knew it was a fact. There were prostitutes living on North Fuller and Hillside, there were prostitutes living on North Gramercy and Garfield Place. I saw them walking into their houses late at night as I drove, holding a man's hand behind them, buzzing people up from their windows. I knew about them but they didn't know about me.

Mary was waiting outside for me. She told me the ladder was in the garage. I told her I had never done this before. She said it was okay, her husband always used to do it and it was just a matter of getting up the ladder and balancing while you took out the leaves. Anyone could do it, really. The old man down the street, if she wanted him to, he'd do anything for her, she said. Anything. But, she wanted *me* to do it. I asked her if she preferred if I vacuum her rug inside. She thought about it for a moment and decided I could do that too.

"I like your hair but I looked better in it."

I looked at her white. She didn't look better than me anymore. I continued to climb up the ladder I had found in the garage, graying wood and water-damaged. I wasn't sure if it would hold me.

"Should I wear gloves or something, Mary?"

"I don't have any," she called up to me.

There were shards of sharp, dry leaves in the gutters, dead bugs, sticks, candy wrappers, things I couldn't even name. At first I took them in between my thumb and forefinger, dropping them slowly below me, on top of her, into her eyes.

"Watch it," she screamed, and went inside.

She left before I could say sorry. I stared down the length of the gutter and knew taking pinches of the debris would keep me up here all day long. The sun was hot and burning on my neck and I leaned over to look deep into the gutters. Didn't she have someone to hire?

"I've got some Indian nickels for you!" She stared up at me, smile wide, holding the faded nickels up at me. I thought about sending a pinch down into her eyes again and decided not to.

When I finished cleaning out the gutters I felt an itch on my arms and decided to ignore it. I climbed down the ladder and focused more on the burning on my neck and back.

Mary let me into her house. Her vacuum was already out, waiting for me.

"I gotta sit down, Mary. I need a drink."

She shuffled into the kitchen and returned with a scotch on the rocks. "I didn't know if you took one cube or two."

I stared at her. Water is what I wanted, but scotch seemed to be the only thing she had.

"Did you see the shrine to my honey?"

In the corner of the kitchen stood her wedding picture. The front of her dress pulled up to show off her legs, her boxer-faced husband smiling at his red-haired siren. There were other pictures too. Him older, on a leather recliner with a plaid shirt on. I never wanted to see him as an old man. I wanted to keep the young, strapping man in my mind. I wondered why she didn't want to keep thinking of him as the young man she once had.

I looked around her house. "What's in there?" I pointed to the closed wood-paneled screen.

"His room. I haven't cleaned it."

"Where do you sleep?" I asked.

"In there."

I stumbled over this for a moment. Why did she call it his room first? I wanted to see it but I knew she would never let me. It seemed sacred. It seemed like things happened in there that I would never be able to find out for myself.

"He treated me like a princess."

I became acutely aware that my arm itched more and more. I looked down at it. Red bumps had started to form. I showed them to Mary. She waved them off.

"My love cleaned those gutters all the time, never a scratch."

"I know, but maybe something's up there."

"Not possible." She went into the kitchen with my glass and came back with a refill. "Two cubes. You look like two cubes."

All I wanted was water but I couldn't bring myself to ask so I gulped down the scotch.

"You have to sip, honey."

"I'm sorry, Mary."

"I get lonely here. No one gives a fuck about me."

I wanted to tell her I cared, but my arm itched and the fear of what it was kept me from really, really caring. She did this to me. Her gutters. A man's job put on me. I only knew her from bingo and I didn't need this. I hoped she didn't want me to vacuum too.

"Do you need a boom box?"

I thought about it for a moment. "No, I don't think so."

She looked around the room from her perch in the recliner, her husband's recliner. "Do you know any men who need clothes?"

I only knew a handful of men, Lev, the desk clerk, and Room 214. Greg. I didn't think they'd want to wear a dead man's clothes.

"He had such nice clothes. I have to give them to someone."

"Goodwill?"

"Then they could end up anywhere. You know what quality these pieces were? Suits like you've never seen. He kept things nice."

I smiled and tapped my glass. "I bet."

"Well, I'll give you the boom box, if you want. But not the clothes. I need to know where they end up."

I got up and asked to go to the bathroom. She pointed down the hall, past the room. I wanted to push in the screen but I knew better.

The hall had more paintings of horses and ships sailing, bad prints of bad paintings, old paintings, and I knew if I moved them the wallpaper would stand out bright against the rest of the fading paper. The walls faded from the sun and age.

"Oooh, my honey loved horses. He was buried with the best of the horse pictures. I only left myself a few. He loved the horses. I made him a wake that you wouldn't believe."

She sighed.

"He bet horses. He sure did. People were after him." She waved her hand at me, screwed up her face. "You *know.*"

"Oh yeah, Mary?" I said. She never talked badly about him. This was a first. She made a lip-zipping motion and I knew it wasn't going to happen again.

"I spent my money, honey. I did it right. I didn't burn him up like those fucks who live across the street. Catholics don't burn their dead. We have respect. He said, he begged, 'Don't burn me up.' And I didn't, honey. I would never."

She waved her hand at me and I thought about what she was saying. We laid out our bodies too. I walked into the bathroom.

"This is the house Jack built!" she yelled at me as I walked down the hall, away from her.

"What?" I asked, turning.

"This is the house that Jack built! It'll be here long after me. They don't make 'em like this anymore, honey. My father didn't use one piece of cheap material on here."

"I see that, Mary," I said and disappeared into the bathroom. I could hear her talking about her father, Jack, as I closed the door.

Inside her bathroom nothing seemed clean, there was a yellow ring around the toilet bowl, dusty rose soaps in seashell shapes, a grime of white haze on the glass shower doors, spots on the mirror and fogging at the sides. It made my face look distorted and I knew why Mary drew her arched eyebrows askew.

It made me feel for Mary and I didn't want to come out of the bathroom and face her. But I did and when I came out she had cobbled together a gift bag for me – a stuffed leopard, a perfume something by Coty – I couldn't make out the faded label, and a three-pack of eye shadows. Long strips of blue and pearl pink and silver. The plastic cover was fogged up and a gold French-sounding name was engraved on the cover.

"The leopard made me think of you. Keep it."

I thanked her and realized that she wanted me out. "Do you need help with anything else, Mary?"

"I need to do my exercises." She shuffled past me and opened the wooden screen door to the bedroom. She creaked it closed behind her.

I heard her turn on an exercise video. A woman with pep called out to stretch your legs and shake out your arms. It was muffled behind the door but I could hear it.

I DROVE BY THE TWIN PALMS AND SAW LEV

snuffing out a cigarette on the sidewalk. He ground it down deep with the heel of his shoe and looked up at me, and I slowed down. He looked surprised, I decided, and happy. I rolled down the window and smiled at him.

"Anka, I like it," he said.

He pulled at my hair and I just smiled. He didn't say any more about it.

"You going home?"

"Yes," I said.

"I come by when I'm done."

"Done with what, exactly?" I smiled at him but he didn't smile back. He turned and ground the cigarette down under his heel.

I drove away without an answer and watched him in my rear-view mirror as I turned off Fairfax.

The house needed to be cleaned, my underwear changed. I checked down there to see the state of things and was unhappy. I turned on the shower, plucked my eyebrows furiously and tried to keep my hand from shaking too much. He hadn't specified when he'd come, but I knew he would. I tapped my fingers on my brow, tapping away the redness and closed the shower door behind me, careful not to wet my hair in the scalding water. I did what I could shaving, trying to look effortless but purposeful.

I knew that he had a wife, but what else did he have? A wife I could deal with.

Maybe.

I laid out my clothes, a push-up bra. In the light I noticed the cream color was a dull shade of gray. I had been wearing it so often and not washing that it had taken on a different tone. I considered the time he'd be here, the light filtering into the room. If this shade of gray, dirt, dry skin, sweat, was acceptable. If I wore a dress or a skirt and he could touch my legs and in between my legs he wouldn't notice the soiled push-up bra. I looked for the best choice of skirt and chose a black mini, black v-neck shirt tucked in.

LEV DIDN'T KISS ME WHEN HE CAME IN. HE

stood in the doorway and asked me where I wanted to go.

I didn't think we were going to go anywhere. This was a new thing.

"I don't know," I said, unprepared.

"I know a Polish place. I bet you miss your own food."

He was walking to his car before I could say, no, I didn't want that. I didn't miss it.

There were two – *Warszawa* was upscale, new Polish. Or the other place, in Eagle Rock. He chose the one in Eagle Rock. A strip mall, where no one would see us. Parking was difficult in front of the dry cleaners. On the glass windows of the place, big red letters said "Nutritious Polish Dishes" in cursive. And then, below it, "*Smaczne Obiady!*"

It wasn't anything like the Twin Palms and it made me ashamed. He pushed me forward and I opened the glass door. A tinkle of the bell alerted the owners that we were there and I wished that I had had an answer for him when he asked me where I wanted to go.

Inside was cramped, booths were crammed next to each other, the inside of the place filled with cheap tables and plastic floral tablecloths. The walls were cubbies filled with dust-covered artifacts from Poland. Blue and white plates with dots and ducks, Polish flags with eagles, everything red and white and fake-royal looking. People hunched over their full plates of food. It smelled like dill and boiled potatoes and Lev looked around and I didn't want to look at him, I just stared at the walls. Pope John Paul II in a gilded frame, the Black Madonna nearby, beer steins from Gdańsk, dried flowers pressed into frames and looped into woven, matted straw-sewn vases.

My face grew hot. This was like the mobile homes on the side of the highway in Poland – tucked in the woods. Frequented by truckers and the young girls from Moldavia and Romania who would bend down over their laps in the cabs of the trucks. Fumbling and sucking. Those roadside restaurants had one picnic table outside and a tilting smoke stack shooting through the roof – homemade. This place was no better. Just bigger. And with Mexicans cooking the food. Dusting the potatoes with dill.

The owner greeted us with open arms.

"Please, come in, table for two right here and for you."

The owner pushed the plastic menus toward us and I stared down at the choices. A small girl ran around the tables. He beamed at her and smiled at us.

"My daughter, Barbara."

He had a thin comb-over, long and tucked behind his ear, a thin mustache, sweat cradling his brow, a checked shirt tucked into his pants. His wife looked up from the window of the kitchen. She was much younger, close-cropped curled hair. When she smiled I could see the metal wires glinting from her canines, her teeth long pulled out and put in fake, like they did in the village, and I knew how she had come here. She went back to making the salads, covered in sesame seed Asian dressing. I didn't know why and Lev didn't ask as he forked around the lettuce leaves, moving around the julienned carrots.

I HAD HEARD ABOUT HIM, THIS MAN, THE

owner of *Solidarność*. He had been a truck driver once, up and down the highways of Poland, past the women standing in the trees from Moldavia, Estonia, waiting to be picked up, to make some money, they stood away from the hunched-over *babcie* selling dried mushrooms along the road. They looked young, 15 or 16, tired and worn-through. I decided that the owner had stopped for them. More than once. He came here and drove trucks again, talking about his exploits, how to please a woman. What to do after hours on the road, how to clean up and smell good. How to open her legs and go down on her. I watched his mouth as he spoke to us, smiled at us, and told us about the specials. I knew this is why he made the restaurant familiar to him. Roadside familiar. Young-girl familiar.

His young wife, almost my age, came over and smiled at us, flour covering her hands, and they stood next to each other like father and daughter and I thought about his mouth on her and I didn't want to eat anymore. Lev pored over the laminated menu and asked for a vodka. The owner said, "I bring it special here from Poland."

I knew it was from plastic jugs bought at Ralph's. That he poked a plastic funnel into Polish vodka bottles and poured in the Ralph's brand, passed it off as authentic and no one knew better. He talked about the aphrodisiac properties of the Żubrówka, how the bison grass made you virile. Lev gulped down the vodka and asked for another. "You don't have anything better?"

"This is the best, from Poland," the owner said, nearly breathless.

"It's shit," Lev said.

Lev thought a moment and asked if they had Stolichnaya.

"We don't carry cheap brands here. Only Chopin. Only Żubrówka."

I wanted to ask him about the economy-sized garbage cans full of empty plastic jugs of Ralph's brand vodka in the back alley, but kept my mouth shut. I was concerned about my need to defend Lev over my own kind. Why instead I felt an urge to shame him, and emasculate him.

The owner walked away and I looked at Lev.

"Why the face, Anka? These are your people. Your place."

I didn't want to tell him that I didn't want this anymore.

The owner brought us more vodka. He asked us what we wanted to eat. He pitched us the *Królewski* Platter – pierogi, *gołąbki* (cabbage stuffed with meat and rice), and *gulasz*. It didn't sound like a royal platter to me. Potato and cheese pierogi, sauerkraut and mushroom pierogi, pierogi with meat.

"What are you going to order?" I asked.

Lev grunted and drank his vodka. They brought us soup. *Żurek*. Potatoes, oily bits of bacon, the sour rye taste and smell. He slurped it up and kept his head down. I looked around at the other non-Polish patrons. They thought this is what we were like. The dusty, dirty shelves of eagles and ceramic red and white sculptures. Salad with sesame seeds. I'm sure they were laughing at this version of us, with all its kitsch and old-world charm. I was embarrassed that the owner pushed it this far. I felt a sense of pride and shame all at once. I felt like I had to tell them how it really was, but then, I didn't really know at all.

The owner came back over and pushed us for our order.

"*Bigos*," I said. Hunter's stew. I looked at Lev slurping his vodka.

We sat and ate in silence. I wondered why he wanted to come over if he wasn't going to speak to me. He ate his royal plate, moved the *gulasz* into his potatoes and left the pieces of meat there, the sauce soaking up the mash.

My mouth tasted sour from the *bigos*. Caraway seeds stuck between my teeth, my tongue could feel them but I didn't want to reach up to the mirror and pick them out in the car, in front of Lev, as he drove back to my apartment.

He said something to me to make me smile and I did, mouth closed, tightly, trying to keep my lips pressed over my teeth, over the seeds. He turned back to driving and I went back to staring straight ahead.

"How is your wife?" I decided to ask.

Lev drove, turned on the radio, a Russian station. Russian pop songs, it sounded like. He turned it up loud, so he couldn't hear me anymore. I listened to the girl singing wildly and wondered what she was singing about, if I would care if I could understand her.

WHEN WE GOT BACK TO MY APARTMENT I FELT

ashamed for where we went. It was low class. He wouldn't quite look at me and I thought it was because of what he saw, and saw in me. This place had made it seem like we were beneath them. It was what I was thinking and I knew he was thinking it too. I went to the bathroom and waited for several minutes and watched how I moved in the mirror. Sucking in my stomach and blowing it out. Fixing my brows, my hair, covering the thin line of light roots growing in. I heard him shuffling around out there and didn't want to go out but I couldn't stay in here. I turned the water off and on, flushed, pulled my panties down and checked to make sure I was clean and good smelling. I sprayed perfume down there and pumped some moisturizer in my hand, perfumed like the spray I had just sprayed, with a hint of glitter, and rubbed it down there too. Just in case.

LEV OPENED MY LEGS UP AS I SAT ON THE

sofa, they shook in his hands. I couldn't help it.

My skirt was working.

My legs looked dewy and fresh from the glitter cream.

I still felt ashamed but I wanted him to want me again, to erase what he had seen and start over. As he got down on his knees and moved the coffee table, he pulled my legs toward him, moving my ass to the edge of the seat and closer to his mouth.

He pushed the folds of my skirt up and his mouth down. I leaned back and tried not to think about anything else. I tried not to think about comb-overs or Polish regal eagles or dust-covered shelves. Lev looked up at me from where he kneeled and I made a face like I liked what he was doing and I wanted it.

Did Lev get on his knees for his wife?

I WATCHED HIM SLEEP ON THE SOFA, MOUTH

gaping and hot, sour air coming out. I went and washed my mouth, my hands, and my face. I brushed my tongue thoroughly. And waited. Lev didn't wake up right away. He moved several times, I thought this time he would open his eyes, but he didn't. I went and cleaned my room. Took my sheets off my bed, newly purchased and already soiled. I turned the mattress over, feeling nostalgic.

The stain was brown by now, years old, like a body had bled out on it. I remembered waking up in it, staring at the red on my legs, still fresh. Redder than anything I had ever seen before. A new kind of blood, from somewhere deep inside of me, that I was unfamiliar with. It was a quick decision but I liked to keep the reminder. The finality was comforting. I had put my head back down on the pillow, closed my eyes and hoped that my panties would stop feeling that wet stick to them.

I got up and stared down at the drying blood on my legs. Walked into the bathroom and was careful not to drip on the white nubby bathmat.

The cleanup was slow. I tried soaking my underwear in cold water and soap, like my mother had taught me when I was younger, careful not to waste any underwear, letting them go until the elastic stretch creaked and fell limp. The cold water and soap didn't work, the blood and water went down the drain and when it was all gone, only streaks of rusty red-brown were left on the cheap porcelain. The underwear would have to go. I threw it in the garbage, a garbage without a top, in a tight-fisted ball and covered it with toilet paper, hoping anyone who came in before I threw away the bathroom garbage would not know to look for it. I washed the sink, kept my bloody legs still and finally took off my shirt and ran the water of the shower, watched it all go down the drain as I stepped inside and scrubbed.

The bed was more difficult. The mattress was sodden red, now a deep brown. I had a bottle of hydrogen peroxide and poured it over, watching the blood sizzle and bubble, the disinfecting seeming to work. I rubbed at it, the red was turning a thin, faded brown and the hydrogen peroxide spread it into a wider swatch of stain. I kept the mattress and stain and it was what I liked to hold on to.

Here it was, still a faded brown, beige at the edges, water-stained and dirty looking. I pulled the mattress up and over again, hiding it. Put the dirty sheets back on. I left the bedroom and sat down next to Lev, hoping I'd wake him with my breathing, with small noises I was making, but nothing made him stir.

WHEN I WATCHED HIM SLEEP, LEV LOOKED

harmless, like a boy. He looked like every other man I had ever watched sleeping. Childish and small. He opened his eye at me.

I got up to move and his hand pulled me back down. "You watch me sleep."

"Sometimes."

"I don't like it."

"You're so paranoid."

"Watch your mouth, Anya."

It was the first time he'd ever spoken to me like that. I looked at him to see if he was joking. He was not.

I said all right and tried to move away. I wanted to get away from him but he wouldn't let me.

He pulled me close to him and kissed me with his sour mouth. I tasted myself on his lips and thought about him kissing his wife with my taste on his lips. If he would wash his mouth out first, if he would wash his face, and then kiss her or if she was used to tasting other women on his lips. If they kissed at all.

"I have clothes in my car; can I bring them in?" he asked.

"To stay here?"

"I could go somewhere else, I think."

I thought about the possibility of Lev. Here, at length. His mouth on me often.

"It's okay. You can stay," I said. He got up and walked out the door. Leaving the door open, letting the streetlight glow and the night sounds come in.

He brought suits in, sharkskin looking things; there was a sheen to them but they still looked cheap. A suit with pin stripes. I thought there might be something going on at the Twin Palms but I was afraid to ask.

"I'm going out but I'll be back in a while," he said.

"Where?"

"Nowhere. Just stay here and wait for me."

And now I would be the one waiting for him, wondering where he was. He didn't change. He left with his rumpled shirt, collar open, pants creased and parts of me drying into the weave.

I would run while I waited for him. I could see my street from where I was running, be able to track his car coming down Fairfax, and watch him walk up the stairs to my house. I let him go and I tied on my sneakers. It was dark already but I knew the lights would be on around the circle, the theater nearby just letting out and there would be people on the sidewalk. I could watch them all, look out for Lev and be able to see the green gaping mouth of the Twin Palms.

Small children were playing soccer on the side of the track. They bounced against each other, kicked up dirt and chased after the ball. I didn't see parents anywhere. I just saw shopping carts overflowing with people's things, covered in blue tarp and next to men and women, a few at most, lying in the grass, watching too. I hadn't seen them before, when I ran, the track was clean and bright during the day. I ran in circles watching the children, my street, everything I was supposed to look out for and averted my eyes from the things I did not want to see. Drunk girls walking up the street. They didn't look ethnic, they did not look like they belonged in the Twin Palms. The sweat was creasing my makeup, I could feel it, and my mascara stung my eyes. It was an unfortunate mistake. I ran harder, contemplated rubbing my eyes, deepening the sting and making them burn red and bright. The lights of the track made the ash look neon white falling down. I breathed in the smoke while I ran, liking the sting and the burn, how I couldn't catch my breath. I felt throw up coming up my throat but I swallowed and kept it down. I let it fill up in my mouth first, cover my tongue, taste the hot sour of Lev and then I swallowed it back down. I did not want to get rid of him, to leave him on the side of the track in the yellowing grass and dirt and pebbles.

AFTER LEV LEFT I FOUND THREE GRAY HAIRS

along the part in my hair. They stuck straight up, more rigid than the rest. I took tweezers and plucked them out. The bulb of the hair follicle still attached. How were they gray? Already? I had heard that men and women grayed down there and I pulled down my pants to check. I took a mirror and placed it down on the bathmat, stood over it and looked for gray hairs. There were moles I had never seen before, skin hung down lower than I had noticed before. I did not like looking at myself. It looked strange, not mine. Discolored. Is this what Lev looked at when he kneeled in between my legs? How could he want to stay?

I did not find any gray hairs.

I put the mirror away and my clothes back on. I rubbed blush on my cheeks and looked at myself in the mirror. How many *in between legs* had Lev seen? Was mine better than the others? How would I know?

The American men I had frequented always said it was the best they'd ever had, the most beautiful, but they still left. If I was aware of the rules ahead of time, this time, things would be different, no? I knew the variables now as I had never known them before. It would be okay, I thought.

THE SHADES WERE DRAWN IN THE GLASS CUBE

of the office and I wondered who authorized the change – to be invisible to the traffic flowing down each side of the boulevard.

I walked in and there was a man standing at the desk. Prim and slim and Pakistani, I think. Middle-aged. It stopped me for a moment but I regained my composure. He smiled at me like he was supposed to.

I walked to the bank of brochures next to the entrance and fingered them, flicking the tops, pulling out ones for Havasu and Laughlin.

"May I help you?" he asked.

I breathed deep. *Where is the desk clerk, Jason,* I wanted to ask, *Who are you,* I wanted to ask.

Was room 214 occupied? Where was Greg?

"How much is a room for the night?" I asked, instead.

The man checked his motel register. He had a thin black mustache and his hair was parted at the side, letting the small tufts near his ear fluff up and out.

"It's 129 for the night," he said.

"That's ridiculous," I said.

He seemed taken aback. "That's the weekend rate, best on the boulevard." He had a lilt to his voice. I could tell he was trying to make a hard sell.

"What about room 214?"

He looked at the key fobs behind him.

"Available." He looked me up and down. "Best room."

"Can I see it?"

"Trust me."

"I want to take a quick look," I said.

He contemplated it and then got sidetracked with a phone call. He was giving someone else the same speech.

I went back to looking at the brochures and considered what to say next. I didn't want to be rushed.

"I was here a few nights ago and I forgot something in one of the rooms. Where's that other guy?"

"Other guy?"

"The one who works here, usually."

"I've been working here for days. I don't remember seeing you."

"Maybe it was last week," I said.

"What did you forget, ma'am?"

"It's private," I said. I was getting impatient. "The other guy said on the phone I could come back and he'd let me in the room."

"Ma'am, I'm the only one here."

"I'm not a *ma'am*." I was clutching onto shiny, slick brochures, printed cheaply and folded precisely. I was bending the edging to them. Stuffing them in my purse.

"What?" He eyed me strangely.

"I'm a *miss*, not a ma'am. Jason. He told me to come back."

"I don't know anyone named Jason."

"Don't you clean the pool?" I said.

"No one's been swimming since the fires."

I knew that wasn't true.

"I left it in room 214."

I made the saddest face I could and he pulled at the fob, annoyed.

I put more brochures in my purse and walked out, behind him.

We walked past the pool, up the stairs and I waited, tapping my fingers on the stucco as he tried to jangle the door open.

He finally opened it. I walked past him and saw the room was empty. Same flower comforter with the plastic sheen. A faint acrid smell, maybe smoke. Nothing else. I pulled the drawer open. The pen, everything was gone. He had the list.

I told the man it was gone and rushed out. He called out and asked if I still wanted the room. I said I didn't have any money and he swore at me in another language. I didn't mind because I didn't know what he said.

I walked up the boulevard, past the Ralph's. The only place to go was home. Back to wait for Lev.

LEV DIDN'T COME BACK UNTIL I WAS ALREADY

sleeping, glass of whiskey and lemon juice and soda next to my bed, near my nose, close enough for me to smell it and turn my stomach while I tried to sleep. Bits of lemon floated up to the surface, hazy brown like swamp water with lemon seeds clustered at the bottom. The knocks were booming and insistent, like I remembered them to be.

I got up and walked to the door, slowly, making him wait, waiting to hear more insistent knocking, to know how badly he wanted to get inside.

They didn't come.

I hesitated opening the door, worrying he had left to try a door somewhere else. When I finally did I saw him sitting in his car, about to turn it on. He saw me and stopped. He got out, pulled the keys out while standing. He walked over to me, pulled his pants up over his stomach and looked left and right, making sure no one was watching, watching him try again and take me up on coming inside.

"Where were you?" he asked.

"Sleeping."

"It's early," he said.

I didn't know what time it was but I didn't think it was early at all.

"Where were you?"

"Nowhere, really."

He said some things in Russian, looked at me, like he didn't want me to be his wife, or his keeper, someone who asked him questions. So I stopped and let him through the door. He walked to the bedroom, pulling off his tie, to my sheets and my mattress hiding my stain and I didn't think he'd ever be in the position to find out about what he was sleeping on. I followed after him, locking the door, and lay down next to him. In between the smell of the glass and the smell of his breath, both heavy with booze and both making my stomach turn. He didn't lean over to kiss me and I hoped that he would turn over, mouth away from me, before he fell asleep. He didn't. He pulled me close to him. Face pressed into his chest, I could barely catch my breath while closing my eyes. I regulated my breathing so that I could lie still, lie quietly, and not suffocate. When Lev had asked me to sleep here I thought it would be different. I thought we would do things besides sleep. His grip was hurting my back and I wanted to move but I knew I couldn't. I closed my eyes and begged myself to fall asleep.

IT HAD BEEN DAYS AND I WAS TIRED OF HIM

already. All I did was open doors for him. Let him out. He hadn't opened my legs in days.

When he came at first I thought, I win.

But he left graying socks with a hole in the toe everywhere, or faded black ones, and I could see the stitches his wife had probably sewn herself. Green thread against the faded black. I wasn't going to do that for him; I hope he didn't expect me to. Maybe that was the part I was missing. I did not know how to sew or knit or darn socks. My mother hadn't taught me anything. When she tried I broke the needles on the electric sewing machine, sending them shooting all over the room. The little yellowing light of her refurbished machine glared down bright on my fingers as I tried to push the fabric through. The hood covering the little light bulb had cracked and broke before we had gotten it and the bare bulb shone in my eyes, making it impossible to thread the tip of the needle. I licked and sucked at the edge of the thread, tried to make it a point but it never worked. She pulled it away from me, put in a new needle and threaded it all in one motion.

"Zosia, you have to learn these things," she said as she pushed the fabric under the needle and pressed her foot down on the pedal that was connected to a cord that connected to the machine and sat under the dining table. She pushed down on the pedal and the sound of whirring and a sound like chomping came out of the sewing machine puncturing over and over.

But it was something I would never learn, and could never do, not even now.

I would not be able to darn Lev's socks, sew buttons back on to his shirt after they popped off, through my carelessness or his. He would always need his wife for that. The way my father needed my mother.

I found Lev's hair in the bathtub, sticking to the drain cover, not making it through the holes. The soap had filmed up against it and turned it an ashy color. I thought about picking it up, and did. The dry soap flaked off in bits and sifted down onto the white porcelain of the tub. It was in a clump and I didn't know where the hair had come from. His head, his crotch, or some other woman, left behind on him somewhere. He wasn't home then, he was somewhere else and I was cleaning up for us. I felt the hair in between my fingers and it crumpled at first, felt coarse, but when the film of soap flaked off it was soft again, stiff and soft and I rubbed it between my fingers and thought about smelling it, but didn't. I put it in the garbage instead. I covered it with unused toilet paper and crumpled it to make it look natural. Like garbage.

Lev came home late, about one or two in the morning. The first few nights I stayed in the living room to wait for him. Watching TV shows and drinking Żubrówka at first, Bison Grass Vodka – hoping it really was the aphrodisiac everyone promised it would be, but Lev wasn't looking for that when he came home. He'd go in the bathroom and wash his face, pull the water through his hair, stare at himself for a while and then close the door when he'd notice me watching him. I could hear his zipper. His urine hitting the toilet water. Sometimes he didn't close the door and I watched, the arc leaving him and hitting the toilet. Sometimes he flushed and sometimes he didn't. No one flushed in Poland either. Water conservation.

The bathroom in the *blok* my grandparents lived in, my parents lived in, and I was born in, always smelled like urine. The pipes were hot and sweating, linking each bathroom on top and below to one another. My grandmother's old washer was crammed in next to the tub, open faced and with a metal washboard that vibrated loudly when turned on. I sat in the tub for hours, inhaling the stale urine smell and hearing Polish yelled from above and below, carried through apartments through the vibrations in the pipes. All of the waste from the gray *blok* slid down the pipes and into the basement.

The *bloki* were all the same and still are, now older and more graffitied - swastikas, slurs about soccer teams and words about Łódź that I could not read. Pentagrams too. No one lived in our apartment in the *bloki* anymore. Our moth-eaten sweaters were still in the cabinets. My favorite dresser – each knob an oversized pink-cheeked girl with orange hair and freckles – still there. I used to claw at those faces, pulling them out toward me, talking to them, each round knob too big for my hands, I had to pull them with two hands, and still I couldn't open the drawers, open the pink-faced girl's mouth.

I TRIED MAKING *ŽUREK* FOR LEV.

Recipe for Zurek "Zhurek"
The base for zurek ("zakwas"):
3 cups of rye flour,
small piece of crust from rye bread,
2 minced cloves of garlic,
2 cups of warm water.

I placed the ingredients in a jar, mixed them well, covered the jar with a piece of clean cloth, and let the jar stay in a warm place for 4-5 days, just like the directions told me to. It said, If mold forms on top, remove it before using the zakwas. Mold did form on top and I gagged while skimming the top. I discarded the bread crust and garlic before using.

Zurek
2 cups of zakwas
3/4 lb of white sausage – chopped (or just use polska kielbasa)
1/2 lb of bacon
1 onion – minced
2 cloves of garlic – minced
1/2 cup of sour cream

1 Tbsp of flour
1 bay leaf
2 corns of allspice
5 black peppercorns
1 Tbsp of marjoram

I fried bacon (chopped), added onion, added garlic and sausage (white). I fried it a little more. I added 3 cups of boiling water, added bay leaf, black pepper. I did not have allspice. I cooked for 20 minutes. Added zakwas. Mixed sour cream with flour, added it to the soup and watched the cream bubble up in lumps. I added dry marjoram I bought at the Polish store, mixed the soup well. I brought it to a boil. The recipe said I could also add chopped, cooked potatoes and chopped hard-boiled egg. I did not add egg.

I THINK I MADE IT TOO SOUR. I LET THE BREAD

and rye flour ferment too long. He spit it back up and that was it.

That's when he asked to take me somewhere. I knew I could ask for the Twin Palms now, and he couldn't say no.

"I only want to go to one place," I said, getting bold now. I had nothing to lose – he had lost his luster to me.

Lev looked at me sideways, up and down. "Do you have a dress, *devochka*?"

"I have several." I walked away from him and into the bedroom. I heard the shower turning on. I needed to prepare myself, wash myself, and shave things.

I looked in my closet. Nothing seemed good enough. I knew where we were going.

I hoped I knew where we were going.

I chose something black and low-cut and slipped into the bathroom after Lev to finish getting ready.

When I came out of the bathroom in the dress, Lev turned me around and kissed my neck, gave me goosebumps. How did he do it, every time.

"Heels, Anka. Nice tall ones," he said.

"I know."

I went into my closet and looked for spindle-heeled shoes. The only pair I owned. The only ones that would do and slipped them on my feet. Wondered how I would make it down the uneven pavement to where we were going. My hair was dry and curled. My lips pert and red. My eyes like a cat's. I took a shot of vodka in the kitchen while Lev finished in the bathroom. I washed the glass. Wiped the frozen bottle of my melted-through fingerprints and returned it to the freezer.

Lev took something from his car as I stood on the street. He reached for my hand and I let him. We were walking down the street toward the Twin Palms and my hands were clammy. I ambled down the sidewalk in my spindle-heels. I tried to keep up with him and look sexy and distinct and purposeful all at once.

I was finally allowed in.

There were people standing around the sidewalk at the Twin Palms. I trailed behind Lev. Trying to walk in a way that accentuated my features. What I wouldn't do for one of those long, slim cigarettes in the hands of the women standing there, looking me up and down, checking to see if my teeth were real, if my roots were pronounced, how I walked, if I was pigeon-toed. Why I was with Lev. They turned away quickly. I hoped for a longer look, a longer glare, more curiosity. Lev pulled me up the stairs, toward the mirror and I heard people speaking quickly in Russian and knew that I had made a mistake to come here. I was scared.

Face red, I trailed behind him, and he let go of me at the top of the stairs and slid through the crowd as I tried to keep up with him in my spindle-heels.

He called out to people, they called out to him. Women looked at me for a moment and then back to what they were doing. I didn't gain a second glance. Lev turned to me. Pale-faced.

"Anka, you should go," he said.

I blinked because I did not want to hear it and took it all wrong. So, I said no.

"Anka, you don't understand. It's not right for you to be here."

I said no, again.

"I'm going to take you home."

I walked away and lost Lev in the crowd, focused on the walls, bubbled glass with a light show reflecting off of it, and being in the Twin Palms for the first time.

The walls were mirrored and shimmery silvery-gold curtains were laced open to more mirrors. There was a mural of New York City on the wall behind the dance floor. The skyline was poorly painted and flaking off in places. There were stained glass windows up here, fading out onto the alleyway, the blocks of color in the glass spelled out "Palms" and mismatched green palm trees lined the frame of the glass. I didn't know what the New York skyline had to do with the rest of the décor but I knew it seemed glamorous to them. The carpet was green, dark like a casino might have and long tables shined with iridescent fabric tablecloths. There was food covering every corner. Picked vegetables, kielbasa, herring with sunflower seed oil, raw onions and potatoes, stuffed peirogi and blini with meat and Russian sour cream. Potato salad – I heard someone call it *olivie*. It was just like the kind we made at home, my mother and I. Chopping up eggs, boiled potatoes, pickles, boiled carrots with the skin still on leathery and slipping from the flesh, raw onions, apples, mayonnaise to stick it all together. There was cured tongue and eggplant *ikra*, surrounded by sliced bread and butter. Red and black fish eggs, some small like poppy seeds and shiny, some round and larger. I had slathered red caviar on bread like jam as a child, spit out the salty brine from my mouth and all the adults around me laughed, patted my head, as if they had all gone through it too, once. I moved away from the smell and the shine. I almost fell into a table of fruit boats with layers of cantaloupe, pineapple, and other fruits exotic to Russia.

It was causing me anxiety, the Russian, the people, the smell of everyone mixed with the food. It looked aged, stuck in time, but I knew it was fresh and made especially for them.

It was too much and I started searching for Lev, but couldn't see him anywhere, I was being pushed and shuffled around, not looked at, not noticed. I went to find a bathroom, a reprieve from the smell and the movement and the talking and the fur.

The bathroom smelled of stale cigarettes and I inhaled deeply and wanted to find one. The bathroom attendant stood in front of an overflowing jar of mints and candies with Cyrillic writing and toothpaste and cheap plastic toothbrushes in yellow and red and green. She had Tic Tacs and Sucrets. She did not have cigarettes and she did not speak English. Women were talking over the stalls in Russian and I felt boozy. I wanted to drink more, to steady myself, but instead I put on more red lipstick, I patted it down to matte. I stuck my thumb into my mouth and closed my lips and pulled out slowly, letting the ring of red flatten against my thumb. I rubbed it off with a tissue and gave the attendant a dollar. I patted my forehead and cheeks with another tissue, saw the makeup transfer on the napkin and threw it in the garbage. I heard the toilets flushing and wanted to run out before I had to see them. But I didn't make it in time, blocked by someone else coming inside. A woman with heaving breasts, loose-fitting leopard gauzy fabric over them. I could see the white of her bra, one of those utilitarian models. Torpedo-shaped and thick strapped, a thick band around the back, letting the fat of her back slide up and down around it.

She spoke Russian to me and for a moment I froze, thinking I had made it. I had passed. The other two women came out of the stall and stared at me too. One had lipstick on thick, carrot-colored that she went to reapply. The other looked at me carefully. Again, the barrel-breasted woman spoke to me in Russian and all I could say was, "*Nie rozumiem.*"

"What you say?" she asked me. She slurred it really. I could smell booze on her breath and I knew.

She said something in Russian to the other women, the

women from the stall, and the woman with the Sucrets and Tic Tacs, and I still couldn't understand.

All I heard was the word Lev.

She blocked the door and I looked behind me. There were no windows. No stained glass. Just metal-doored bathroom stalls and the Russian woman applying her carrot-colored lipstick. The other two chattering above me. The bathroom attendant stayed mute.

"Who you come with?" the leopard lady asked me.

The thin woman stood near the mirror with her friend, standing quiet and still. She was wearing a petal-pink suit-skirt and patterned silk shirt. Her shoes were open-toed and revealed swollen toes. She had bunions, I could tell. A hammer toe maybe. The shoes were misshapen and the material jutted out in strange directions. The polish on her toes was old, faded, and shimmery pink, chipping at the tips and her nails were splitting vertically. An old woman's feet.

I wanted to look away but I didn't want to face the barrel-busted woman and her question.

"*Nie rozumiem,*" I said again.

"You don't understand English either?" she asked, low and slow.

I shook my head no and gave myself away.

The thin one spoke, finally. "I saw you come with Lev?" She said it like a question and I didn't know how to respond. So I slowly nodded yes.

"You know him," she asked.

"Yes," I said.

The leopard lady neighed at me, held her drink to her lips and slurped some up.

"That's her husband." She pointed at the thin woman, and her friend stopped applying her lipstick. Her mouth sufficiently orange.

"I don't know what you're saying," I said. They were circling me now and wouldn't let me pass. They were older than me and they could all be my mother, young mothers or grandmothers.

"He has three kids at home. One baby." She trilled the *th* of *three*. She held on to it long, like my mother would. "And two in Moscow."

I wasn't surprised but I wished I could be. I wanted to be.

The thin woman, Lev's wife, glared at me. "What you think, you his first *shluha*?"

I could hear the big one snorting and I knew what was going to happen.

She let loose on me. I felt the warm wet against my scalp. She had spit on me. All of them were doing it. The bathroom attendant continued folding towels and acted like she wasn't seeing it. The others took their turns too. On my face, my neck, the orange-lipped woman got her orange-tinged spit in my ear.

I started hitting them, whoever I could get. I smeared orange across the woman's face. Got it on the palm of my hand. I launched after the leopard tank afterwards. I knocked her in the mouth. Her dentures flew out and left a pink-gummed crevice. She squealed and I saw her Soviet-era teeth break into bits, tooth by tooth on the bathroom floor, sliding beneath the toilet. She covered her mouth and yelped. A gaping-mouthed old woman. She didn't look sinister anymore. She looked old and poor.

Lev's wife looked at me; she had hung back, kept her petal-pink suit tidy and away from my flailing hands. We looked at each other then and I knew I had no right to attack her. She was everything I now realized I never wanted to become. A village girl with wired-in teeth, ruby-colored hair curled tight to her head. She couldn't have been more than 35 but she looked 50. Smoke lines on her face and pink blush layered over loose skin. They were immigrants but they weren't like my immigrant parents. They got married the Eastern European way, I figured. Pregnant while fucking. Then marriage. Then leaving the village.

The leopard lady hunted around the floor for her teeth, each porcelain nub, and I finally could leave. No one was in my way. Lev's wife looked like she wanted to strike me but wouldn't. The woman with the carrot-colored lips was wiping off and starting over, trying to clean up her face.

I pushed out of the bathroom. Lev was standing there, waiting for me. He looked fraught, scared for the first time. He was saying things like, *Devochka, are you okay*, things like that. He tried to pull me away from the door, with him, but I just pushed past him.

Out of the Twin Palms.

I broke my heel leaving, heading down the carpeted stairs with their thin fading flowers in red and pinkish hues on the green background. The spindle broke but I had a strong grip on the railing and only stuttered forward. People pushed past me and up the stairs, to where they belonged. I walked slowly down the sidewalk, away from the Twin Palms and on the ball of my right foot, balancing out the left.

I passed stores with neon sturgeons in the window and *CAVIAR* written in neon cursive inside the belly of the fish. Pawnshops with dirty, faded gold rings in the windows. The window said, "WE BUY GOLD." Women's rings lined the plush-holed display cases, everything looked worn out, faded down, and I didn't want to look anymore.

Smoke was billowing behind the hills in front of me. And the light was fading against a line of palm trees, bright blue and then glowing orange in the distance. There were two places I could go to get a better look and I weighed my options. The top of the canyon had coyotes, homeless men in the bushes; that's what I believed anyway. Griffith Park was the other. The observatory. I wasn't sure what could be there. I had heard several things.

I stopped at home first, wiped my face off, and took my dress and my shoes off. Threw all of it into the garbage and I changed into things that needed to make sense to me again. Pants, sneakers, a t-shirt. I took any remnant of Lev that I could find, his clothing, a gold ring, a comb, and shoved them in another bag and took it with me. I looked up at the sky as I was leaving, at the power lines where the birds used to sit, gone and quiet now, and up past the palm trees to see the smoke creeping forward.

I had to park on the street because the gate was closed.

The park looked long and dark and I had begun to believe this was a bad idea but I needed a better look at the city. I had been trawling the boulevards and avenues, *the flats*, and I needed to see things. Bright things.

At the mouth of the park I could still hear cars. Honks, the whirring of motors, fits and starts of traffic on Los Feliz Boulevard. I walked into the darkness and wished I had thought of bringing a flashlight. I heard bird noises, rustling noises, noises that were unfamiliar and unsettling. I walked further, where the park lights stopped shining, on the road twisting up the hill. There were probably coyotes here too. I could smell jasmine and the fires made the city warm, but pockets of cool air slipped over me as I climbed up, deeper into the dark. When I heard unfamiliar sounds, park sounds, I stopped and listened, my skin tingling, my spine feeling tense.

Then things became quiet. I hadn't heard this kind of quiet before, dark quiet, empty quiet. The only thing to do was to keep moving. It took a while and when I reached the top I had sweat through my shirt and my upper lip was wet with perspiration. My bag felt heavy on my shoulder and I thought I had been walking for an hour. The air had made my chest heave, my hair probably smelled like smoke.

When I reached the top of the spiral, I could see the parking lot of the observatory, and it was empty. Lit up and glowing, and from up here the ash was really coming down, a blizzard of it, whirring in circles. I couldn't see the grid yet. The trees slouched toward the parking lot and obscured the view. I had to get closer. There was a dirt walkway on the side of the building and as I walked down, the city opened up beneath me. Blue squares lined the flat and intersected forever. I was sweating and breathing heavy and needed to collect myself. Here it was.

Los Angeles.

I didn't know what to say or do so I just sat quietly on a rock, wiping the sweat from my face with the sleeve of Lev's dress shirt, sticking out of my bag. There weren't any fires in this direction but the glow of the sky was orange. The buildings jutted from the landscape and I just sat there, ash crinkling down around me. This city was cut up into neat squares. Avenues were dissected by boulevards which were dissected by streets and I wanted it all to mean something to me. I wanted to understand. I tried looking for my apartment. My alley. The Twin Palms. I sat there and studied the landscape, followed Los Feliz Boulevard to Sunset Boulevard to Fairfax Avenue and down. Down to where I was supposed to be and to where Lev might be.

IT WAS CLEAR TO ME THEN THAT THERE WAS

no way out. Greg was right. The neat and tidy squares couldn't contain us anymore. The blur of blue and orange streetlights, the throb of cars snaking out of the city. They were crushing each other to get out. The highways were flooded with automobiles and I realized there was no way out. The glut was going to keep us in here forever. There was nothing to go to anyway. There was desert to the east of us, water to the west. North was the Grapevine and mountains that were burning. Los Angeles was trapped and I was trapped within it. And neither of us should have been here in the first place. The fires, the mudslides, earthquakes. Why didn't anyone see that we didn't belong here anymore, ever? I jumped up. I had parts of Lev that would help it along. We would help the purge.

The smell up here was of wood fires and smoke chimneys and cool pockets of air and hot waves of ash and I climbed away from the blinking and away from the observatory and the white glow on the hill and away into the woods. Away from Hollywood and Downtown and over to the valley. To the fires and the smoke and the hills and mountains. That's where I belonged, closer to the ash and closer to the smoke, and fire lapping in the distance. I would add to it, make it bigger and more pronounced. I would finally make my mark. I hoped that Greg was somewhere up here. But he wasn't. Yet.

The fires were closer now. No longer in Simi Valley or the outskirts of the city. I could see rows of red and orange, fire lines down the hills in Burbank and moving closer to us, along the ridges of the mountains. It was uncontainable and shrouded the valley with a thick cloud of smoke, dulling the grids on this side. There were helicopters dotting the sky up and around the fires. Channel 7 and Channel 4 were vying for a better view, trying to get closer to the action. They were circling up there in the sky, moving in zigzag motions, too far from where I was to get the story first. The dirt trail slid down under my weight and I saw the bright white letters floating up and over the ridges of the hill. H-O-L-L-Y-W-O-O-D, the *LAND* long gone. It looked vulgar here in the dark, it looked like a lie.

It didn't matter anymore.

Lev had left his clothes and they provided the perfect kindling. Cologne-soaked, the cheap suit fabric was highly flammable. I draped the pieces over dry brush and lit each corner and watched the flames lick and twist onto themselves. Trying to get bigger. I ran back and forth, lighting all of them.

The flames were slow at first. I didn't think they would even take, or keep. The wind made it hard to light everything and my thumb became worn and bruised while I worked on the flaming. Lev's shirt fluttered in a pile of dirt as the Santa Anas picked up and snuffed itself out. It was frustrating. I took his shirt, inhaled his smell now mixed with a thin stench of smoke and tried lighting it again. This time it took.

I stood back and watched the burn. The Santa Anas pushed the flames left and right, up trees nearby. This would get the glut moving again. This was me making it work.

I COLLECTED FUCHSIA BOUGAINVILLEA ON MY

way down the hill. Tugged at my hair to interlace the blooms with strands of hair and wrapped a branch around me as I made my way down to my car.

By the time I had got there, sirens weren't far off and the petals of the bougainvillea had begun to wither and turn oily to the touch. The sky was growing brighter. I wasn't sure if it was the fire enveloping Griffith Park or the sun rising. The clock in my car had stopped working so there was no way of knowing for sure. All I knew was that it was time to get home.

There was bougainvillea strewn in the middle console and on the carpet beneath my feet. I had fuchsia petals in my hair. I pulled them out with some strands of hair still attached and rolled down my window. Threw it all out at a stoplight, petals under my feet, from the seat next to me. Threw them all over Western.

I wasn't feeling any better.

I WALKED UP THE STAIRS TO MY APARTMENT

and my neighbor, the mackerel-giver, was standing there, smiling at me. I sat down and there was a velvet painting of mountains and trees leaning against the metal grate of my door.

"Have you ever been to New York City?" he said.

I wasn't in the mood for questions or conversation, so I said no.

"My daughter lives there. She's getting married."

I looked at his mustache, curled up over his smile. "You have a kid?"

"Yes, she's getting married." He stood there smiling in plaid shorts and sweat creeping out from the armpits of his shirt.

"Congratulations."

"I was thinking of moving there. Be close to her."

"What's this?" I said.

"My mother wants you to have it. She has no more wall space."

I held it up, the frame was gold flecked, ridged, and molding. The velvet was coarse and had a layer of dirt on it, the paint flecking off in whites and blues but the mountains looked majestic and popped off the velvet. I contemplated keeping it.

"I can't take this," I said.

"You must."

His mother came out onto the balcony, toothless and spangle-scarfed. She looked like a gypsy to me. She smiled and shoved her hands at me. There was no giving it back.

"You should give it to your daughter," I said.

"I'm not bringing it to New York City."

They smiled at me and waited for me to thank them and bring it inside.

I nodded my head, turned the key to my door and said good luck. And thank you.

The apartment was dark.

I put the painting up against the wall and walked into the kitchen. I found what I was looking for and went and nailed the painting to the wall. Or, I nailed a screw into the wall and hung the rusting wire of the frame on it, hoping it would hold. I hung it so you could see it through the sliding glass door, so they could see it. My immigrant velvet painting. I stood back and stared at it. It was the best thing I owned.

My mother would hate it. It was cheap and dated, mid-seventies kitsch. Probably the Ural Mountains. *Uralskie gory.* Or maybe the Tatras. *Tatry Zachodnie.* Why would Russians have a velvet painting of Polish mountains? It didn't make sense. They were the Urals for sure. Lev would like it, I think. I imagined him standing back and laughing, telling me all about the Urals. And then, I realized that would happen so I opened the curtains so the whole street could see my new painting, my gift. I had to share it with someone.

THE CHECKS HAD STOPPED COMING A FEW

weeks before and I knew I would be in trouble. When I walked outside and saw my car was gone, I panicked at first, had the police taken it, did they know? But I was still here, they hadn't come after me, so I knew it wasn't that. Boris from upstairs called down to me. "They took it."

His shirt was stained and had holes in it, and he stuck his plastic shoe through the metal bars of his balcony.

"Who took it?" I asked.

"The truck came and –" He threw his hands up, motioned the rest.

When I exhaled he leaned down further, almost falling over the ledge. "What you going to do?"

"I don't know, Boris." I went back inside and closed the door behind me.

Repossessed, I thought. There was no leaving here now. Just sit and wait for them to come to me, if they were ever going to. I turned on the television. The helicopters on television were echoed by the ones in real life around me. The newscasters were using words like *deliberate*.

I stared at the Urals on my wall and wanted to be there, instead of here. I tried to think cool thoughts. Snow and such. Anything to get away from the oppressive heat surrounding me.

I TURNED OFF MY PHONE, I TURNED OFF THE

lights, and I didn't leave the house for a few days. I ate beans and rice, chicken broth with frozen mixed vegetables and broken pieces of spaghetti, frozen burritos with freezer burn through the plastic, which I found toward the back of the freezer where I never looked.

I found more of Lev's hair. At the bottom of the bathtub, in my sheets. I tried to get rid of it all. I scrubbed the bathtub and the toilet with bleach until my hands burned and my nostrils burned. Until I couldn't smell anymore. I had fine cuts on my fingers and palms from scrubbing with the scouring pad, from rubbing at the bleach. I took my sheets and put them in the washer, in the laundry room with the rubber tube that let the water flow out of the washing machine, into the big molding basin, a rim of hair around the base, and I knew Lev would stay there. His hair mixed in with the others.

I could hear Boris coming down the stairs and I didn't want to talk to him, have him ask me about my car again. Talk about the fires anymore. I turned off the light and crouched next to the bleating machine. It sounded like it was dying and it drowned out my breathing. I could see Boris's head bobbing as he carried his trash to the alleyway. Singing something from Ukrainian television.

And then I could see Lev. He pressed the buzzer several times, then knocked against the metal grate of my door. I guessed he had come back for his things. But I had left them in the park, burning.

I saw Boris coming back around from the alley and Lev spotted him too.

"Where is she?" he asked Boris.

"How should I know?" He continued up the stairs, unafraid of Lev.

He banged on my door a few more times, peered into the laundry room at the shaking machine and tried the door. It was locked and he couldn't see me crouching under the basin, under the dripping water pooling in the sink.

I waited for him to leave and got up when I heard him turn on his car and drive away. He was going back to his wife or to someone else. I didn't care anymore. He wasn't mine. Never was.

I THOUGHT ABOUT WHAT PEOPLE WOULD FIND

in my apartment after I left. What remnants of me would tell them who I was? The television said they were closer to figuring things out. Possible witnesses. I went about searching for things in the apartment.

I found:

1. Strands of different colored hair.
2. "Adamba" brand Polish style *żurek*, like my mother always bought. I had lost count of how many packages I had collected. The front had a lady in a *chustka* and floral apron holding a steaming bowl of soup.
3. Bobby pins. Both mine and the mystery girl from when I had moved in. Separated in two piles.
4. Matches.
5. Several empty boxes of varying types of Misty cigarettes.
6. A bloody mattress.
7. Love notes – to the city and to individuals, that I had never sent.
8. My grandfather's glasses, in their case. The thick bottle cap kind, with lenses that looked like sea glass, almost. His case, a thin, stiff leather. They felt 100 years old.

I HAD FIFTEEN MISSED CALLS AND SEVEN MES-

sages. I didn't think anyone would call and I was keeping a low profile as people like to say. When I checked the messages I confirmed that no one good had called.

My mother left all the messages on Sunday. I knew what it was about. Lent. What was I going to give up? Had I gotten ashes crossed on my forehead. Had I gone to confession? I had done both.

I turned the television on for the first time in several days. The newscasters were on site, ash in their hair. The fire someone had set near the Hollywood sign was spreading and the observatory was already damaged. They were spraying the surrounding homes with water, keeping everything wet, the ground saturated. There were evacuations, but some people didn't want to leave. They were showing a man next to a pool with a surgical mask on. He was pumping pool water in a hose to the sloping hillside. He said, "I've been through fires before and beat them every time." The newscaster had an urgency in her voice, like he was being foolish, like he might not make it if he didn't leave.

I opened the windows to let the air in and the smoke came in huffs. The newscasters played out the scenarios. How to save each letter. How firefighters were stationed around the sign, wetting it cold and damp. Trying to keep it safe. It was going to be a story of saviors, that's how it was playing out now. Heroes were being made right on the television.

There was a knock on my door and I was afraid to open it. I hid back in the shadows of the apartment but could see my neighbor leaning over and trying to peer in through the glass doors. I worried about him jumping the lip of my balcony, seeing if they were open. Why hadn't I closed the blinds? He moved away from the glass and went back to knocking on the front door.

I came and opened the door a little, eyeing him.

"Are you okay?" he asked.

"Fine. Sick."

"My mother made you soup."

I looked at his empty hands.

"She has it on the stove," he continued.

I was wearing clothes that I had not changed for days. I had not showered and I had tufts of hair growing in my armpits. He smiled at me and nodded his head. Saying yes for me.

I kept the door open as I went to look for my shoes. When I came back he motioned to the mountains and said, "It is nice."

Their apartment was built much like mine. Wall to wall oatmeal-colored carpeting, a living room, their sliding glass door, a dark hallway leading to bedrooms and a slim alcove of kitchen to the left, instead of the right, like mine. The blown up photographs of family lineage I had seen through the window were right in front of me now, lining the tops of the wood and glass cases, tacked to the walls in a line all around the tight room. Close up they were fuzzy with dust and yellowing.

They had fit a dining table, sofa, Persian rug, six curved and wooden dining chairs and dozens of black-and-white photos in cheap plastic frames into the front room. I was in a mausoleum smelling of chicken fat and boiling root vegetables. The old woman in the *chustka* came out of the kitchen smiling, holding boiled chicken pieces, tawny skin fat still puckered and goose-pimpled, and thick-sliced pieces of gray boiled beef sitting in a thin sleeve of oily chicken stock. She set it down on the white embroidered tablecloth and dribbled oil on the cloth and went back into the kitchen, ladling soup over thin egg noodles and passing the bowls to her husband, the small hunched man I had seen walking back and forth in front of our apartment building, hands behind his back held together by the thumbs and loose-fitting gray slacks bunched at the waist with a belt. He wore the same square-sided hat atop his head, beaded and sparkled. I wondered if he was wearing it for religion, for some Russian Orthodox reason. I didn't want to ask. The television was blaring guttural fast-talking. When he put the bowls on the table he put himself back in the worn leather chair and his wife set the soup in front of him. He turned the TV louder and I noticed the glazed gaze I often saw when passing by the window. He didn't say a word to anyone and my neighbor and his mother sat at the table, smiling their toothy and toothless grins at me. Waiting for me to slurp the soup and break apart the loose-skinned chicken sitting in front of me. I looked down at my soup, the parsley cut coarsely, floating atop a film of oil and gristle. It smelled delicious. It smelled like the old country. I ate it up quickly and was given seconds. Not even working around the brown and gray bits floating in the broth, I ate those too. They smiled and the mother nodded.

She said, "Good."

I nodded and said, "Very."

Her son smiled at me and said something to her in Russian. They both smiled at each other and then smiled at me. He didn't translate what he said. I kept my head down. Smelling the *rosół* and my own body odor. I would shower when I got home, I decided. I would start fresh. The soup warmed me and made me feel taken care of. They spoke in another tongue, ignored me, and it felt fine.

IN THE SHOWER I SHAVED MY LEGS AND ARM-

pits, looked at the fine hairs on my arms collecting water drops from steam. I foamed my legs and pulled the razor up carefully, cutting through the cream, shaved my pubic hairs, all of them. I cut the lip down there and let out a whimper. It bled into the water, pouring down my legs, and I bit down hard. I had done it before and knew it would take a long time to heal. My hair was washed thoroughly, shampooed twice until my fingers felt no slickness from grease and squeaked clean against the hairs. Next, the conditioning treatment for shine. I left it on for 10 minutes. Longer than necessary. So I shampooed again and hoped the shine would stay. I rubbed soap on and finally turned off the shower, pulled Epsom salts from next to the tub and poured some in my hand, careful not to drop any in the tub, lose any. I scoured my skin, taking off layer after layer. Checking for soft-ness, spending extra time on my kneecaps, elbows, the skin next to my anklebone. I rubbed my toes and my heels and rubbed at my heels until they felt raw, then my fingers and wrists, the part above my wrist bone, pulled salt around the thin blond hairs of my arms and tried to scour the hair away. I rubbed salt on my shoulders, tried to reach my back, rubbed my butt raw, trying to rub the stretch marks away, the same with my thighs, my inner thighs, careful not to get salt into the cut I had given myself while shaving. I had felt the sting before and had not liked it.

My face was last, lightly on the cheeks, forehead, chin. I knew I would be red-faced but I needed to get it all off – smells of him, ash flecks, smells of smoke both from Los Angeles and my cigarettes. I turned the water back on and the spray from the shower pooled all the salt at the bottom of the tub and I watched it go down, turned it hotter, almost scalding, and watched my skin turn red.

Next, I slathered on layers of cream on my freshly raw skin. It felt smooth and new. The roughness washed away with the salt. When I emerged from the bathroom the steam folded off of me and I smelled the burnt smell again. In the bathroom it was gone, just the smell of water and bath products and thick creams and my grime washing away. Now the smell of the fires pulled into the house from the open sliding glass door and I ran to close it.

WITH NO CAR, I HAD TO RELY ON BUSES.

There were no maps at the bus stops. No indication of where to go. I figured each bus went down each avenue, each boulevard toward downtown or off toward the beach. I pointed myself east and rode buses in a maze toward Little Armenia, toward the Church of the Holy Virgin. Toward the fires on the hill in Griffith Park, toward the firefighters coming down in stretches trying to save the white letters stabbed into the hill.

I walked three blocks past the bus stop to get to the Holy Virgin. Mary was standing in front of the church, looking perturbed. "Where you been?"

"I was away," I said.

"You didn't tell anyone." She looked at me annoyed. Started walking away.

"Why aren't you going inside?"

"Canceled. The fires," Mary said.

She stared up at the black cloud of smoke hanging low in the distance and scowled, flicked ash from her hair, nearly pulling out her red rhinestone barrette.

"What's your name again, honey?" she asked. I was hurt for a moment and then I remembered she was old.

"Where's your car?" she asked me. I could only tell her the truth.

She shook her head at me.

"You need to talk to Maria Rosa."

"Who?"

"My psychic. She'll set you straight, tell you what's going to happen."

"I already know what's going to happen," I said.

"You don't know shit." She snorted and pulled at her purse. Black fabric with Betty Boop smiling, the pleather patch ironed on. "I can call us a cab with the money I was going to spend at bingo tonight."

I thought about the money I would lose with bingo being canceled, knowing I would never get my car back at this rate. Mary went inside the rectory and came back minutes later. Her cane bobbing in front of her.

"Five minutes, they said. That means 10." She sat down on the ledge in front of the church.

"There's more and more Filipinos coming to bingo now. They love to gamble."

"Since I last came?"

Mary nodded her head and made a face. "It's an invasion. They love Jesus and they love bingo. I can't even understand them."

I walked over and sat down next to her on the ledge. She was sweating in the heat. Her sweatshirt too thick for the weather. She had drawn her eyebrows in black today and I wondered if she used eyeliner this time, they look arched and furious as she tugged at her cane, licking her lips.

"It ruins my chances of winning."

"They add more money to the pot," I said.

"They call out bingo when they don't even win. Fuck everything up."

"Maybe they'll go away, Mary."

"Eh, they're not going anywhere." She shook her head and looked down the road impatiently. Up and down, leaning forward and checking every few seconds. We'd run out of things to talk about.

"You have 20 dollars?" she asked.

"No. I don't have anything," I said.

She looked in her purse and counted. She had a lot of bills. Too many to carry around. She couldn't fight anyone off, maybe with her cane, but I doubted it.

"This is all I have left," she said.

I asked her what she meant but she didn't respond.

"Where am I supposed to go now that bingo's canceled?" she said.

"Home, Mary," I said.

She snorted. "You have 20 dollars?" she repeated.

"Why are you asking me for money when you have so much?" I asked.

"It's for you, not me," she said.

She stuffed a twenty in my hand. "You can pay me back."

"What's it for?" I asked

"Maria Rosa."

"I don't need to know anymore," I said.

Mary shook her head at me, like I was all wrong.

"I don't want to go to Maria Rosa. I want to go home," I said.

Mary looked at me, long and hard. She gave the cab driver directions and I knew where we were going. The cab stopped at the yellow tape and Mary and I made the rest of the way to her home on foot. Her with her cane, me trying to help.

Her house was charred, but still standing.

"Oh, Mary," I said because I didn't know what else would fit.

"They don't make them like they used to, not like this anymore. This is the house that Jack built," Mary said. She looked lost, like when she was left behind at bingo.

I looked at the house. It was a shell now. The shrine to her husband gone. The saints all gone with it.

"It's still standing though, boy. They don't make 'em like they used to. Those new houses wouldn't have made it," she said.

Mary took out the one picture of her husband she had left, the good luck charm from bingo. Small-framed and silvered.

"The bricks need to be repainted. The stairs fixed," she said.

I kept looking at the house, trying to see what she could see. There was nothing left to fix.

"Where are you going to go, Mary?" I asked.

"Go? I'm gonna stay right here. This is the house that Jack built. My father built it with his hands, his own two hands."

I didn't tell her that I did this to her. Maybe I shouldn't have forced it on her. Maybe she was happy in her grief. After all, it was all she had left.

I LEFT MARY. COULDN'T LOOK AT WHAT I HAD

done any longer. I walked past the yellow tape and down, away from the fires. I went alone. Los Angeles wasn't leaving and I couldn't make it go away.

Instead, I would have to leave it because I had failed to cleanse the desert. The city was resilient and unmoving, undaunted by the smoke clouding all around it, ash gently falling. The sun was setting in the west and it was blood red, large and balloon-like and it felt like a protection.

I started walking. Leaving however I could.

MY FATHER HAD TOLD ME THE STORY ABOUT

when he and my mother had gotten married. A small church in my mother's village. It was where the farmers brought their crops and covered the altar in the fall, begging for a new harvest in the spring. It was next to the graveyard where my family lay. My parents were still young, twenty or twenty-one and my mother was not pregnant. She wore a dress her mother had sewn for her and my father was even younger than my mother. Scared. He said, walking away from the church, through the rye fields, alone and together with no one following them, was the best point of their marriage. Their walk to the train, through the fields of swaying rye and over the tracks to the one train out of their village. He said it twice; this was their best moment together. With the most hope. In the distance, the farmers were already burning their potato fields after picking their crops. The smoke was thick and hung low in the air. They did it neatly, in order to prepare the soil for new growth.

NOTE ON THE COVER ARTIST

RICARDO CAVOLO was born in Salamanca, Spain, in 1982, in a painting studio. Most of his works are paintings and illustrations, but also sculpture and street art.

He has completed illustrations for Cirque du Soleil, Ogilvy, Leo Burnett, AIGA, Urban Outfitters, and magazines all over the world. His art has been exhibited in Spain, Russia, and Switzerland, as well as published in three books.

To see more of his illustrations, find out about exhibitions, and sign up for his newsletter, visit **ricardocavolo.com**, where some of his work is also available as prints or t-shirts.

Also published by **TWO DOLLAR RADIO**

RADIO IRIS
A NOVEL BY ANNE-MARIE KINNEY
A Trade Paperback Original; 978-0-9832471-7-3; $16 US

"Kinney is a Southern California Camus."
—*Los Angeles Magazine*

"A noirish nod to the monotony of work."
—*O: The Oprah Magazone*

BABY GEISHA
STORIES BY TRINIE DALTON
A Trade Paperback Original; 978-0-9832471-0-4; $16 US

"[The stories] feel like brilliant sexual fairy tales on drugs. Dalton writes of self-discovery and sex with a knowing humility and humor." —*Interview Magazine*

DAMASCUS
A NOVEL BY JOSHUA MOHR
A Trade Paperback Original; 978-0-9826848-9-4; $16.00 US

"*Damascus* succeeds in conveying a big-hearted vision."
—*The Wall Street Journal*

"Nails the atmosphere of a San Francisco still breathing in the smoke that lingers from the days of Jim Jones and Dan White." —*New York Times Book Review*

SEVEN DAYS IN RIO
A NOVEL BY FRANCIS LEVY
A Trade Paperback Original; 978-0-9826848-7-0; $16.00 US

"The funniest American novel since Sam Lipsyte's *The Ask*."
—*Village Voice*

"Like an erotic version of Luis Bunuel's *The Discreet Charm of the Bourgeoisie*." —*The Cult*

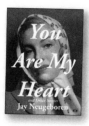

YOU ARE MY HEART AND OTHER STORIES
STORIES BY JAY NEUGEBOREN
A Trade Paperback Original; 978-0-9826848-8-7; $16 US

"[Neugeboren] might not be as famous as some of his compeers, like Philip Roth or John Updike, but it's becoming increasingly harder to argue that he's any less talented... dazzlingly smart and deeply felt."
—Michael Schaub, *Kirkus Reviews*

THE ORANGE EATS CREEPS
A NOVEL BY GRACE KRILANOVICH
A Trade Paperback Original; 978-0-9820151-8-6; $16 US
 * National Book Foundation 2010 '5 Under 35' Selection.
 * NPR Best Books of 2010.
 * *The Believer* Book Award Finalist.

"Krilanovich's work will make you believe that new ways of storytelling are still emerging from the margins." —*NPR*

THE VISITING SUIT
A NOVEL BY XIAODA XIAO
A Trade Paperback Original; 978-0-9820151-7-9; $16.50 US
"[Xiao] recount[s] his struggle in sometimes unexpectedly lovely detail. Against great odds, in the grimmest of settings, he manages to find good in the darkness."
—Lori Soderlind, *New York Times Book Review*

THE PEOPLE WHO WATCHED HER PASS BY
A NOVEL BY SCOTT BRADFIELD
A Trade Paperback Original; 978-0-9820151-5-5; $14.50 US

"Challenging [and] original... A billowy adventure of a book. In a book that supplies few answers, Bradfield's lavish eloquence is the presiding constant."
—*New York Times Book Review*